A MOTIVE EMERGES

Eardley—he's a slimy creature if ever there was one—had discovered irregularities in Richard's life: A relationship with another member of the repertory, a girl called Mary Norton. Apparently they'd been living together for three years. The following week, when Laura confronted Richard with Eardley, Eardley fairly spat out the accusation about Mary Norton. And followed it up with a tirade about the wickedness of stage performances in general and the people who took part in them in particular. And then mentioned the possibility of Richard having to see less of his son. The son that meant more to him than his own life. And maybe more than Laura's life as well.

MURDER'S OUT OF TUNE

Sara Woods

...murder's out of tune,
And sweet revenge grows harsh.
Othello, Act V, scene ii

AVON BOOKS  NEW YORK

Any work of fiction whose characters were of uniform excellence could rightly be condemned—by that fact if by no other—as being incredibly dull. Therefore no excuse can be considered necessary for the villainy or folly of the people appearing in this book. It seems extremely unlikely that any one of them should resemble a real person, alive or dead. Any such resemblance is completely unintentional and without malice.

S.W.

AVON BOOKS
A division of
The Hearst Corporation
105 Madison Avenue
New York, New York 10016

Hilary Term, 1975

Tuesday, 28th January

I

'I cannot think,' said Sir Nicholas Harding severely, eyeing the cigar which he had chosen carefully from the box at his elbow as though he suspected it of some subversive intention, 'why you should commit yourself to visiting foreign parts when there is so much work awaiting you at home.'

His nephew, Antony Maitland, who had just finished a round with the sherry decanter, paused a moment before placing it back on the tray. 'I shouldn't exactly call Yorkshire foreign parts,' he objected mildly. 'As for the work that's waiting for me here, you know that case of Bellerby's is as dull as ditch water, the verdict's a foregone conclusion, and he couldn't care less whether Derek or I deal with it.'

'That may be true.' Sir Nicholas made the concession unwillingly. 'But I still see no reason –'

'Chris is worried,' said Jenny Maitland, interrupting him, a thing she very rarely did. She was sitting curled up in her favourite corner of the sofa, and it was obvious that to her, as well as to her husband, this fact settled the matter beyond argument.

'If Chris is going to call on you every time he has a family crisis –'

'Not family this time,' Antony put in hastily. He thought about that for a moment. 'At least, not exactly,' he added with a certain amount of doubt in his tone.

'Not exactly?' His uncle pounced on the admission and turned to look at his wife despairingly. 'You will agree with me, my dear Vera, that that remark requires some clarification. Unless' – he bent a suspicious eye on his nephew again – 'you are being deliberately evasive, Antony.'

Maitland took a moment to exchange a rather rueful look with his aunt, who responded with a grim smile and said in her gruff, elliptical way, 'Better explain.'

Antony had come back to the fireside now and had taken the wing chair opposite to the one his uncle always used when he visited them. 'I'm going to, of course, as far as I can,' he said. 'But I only know what Chris told me over the phone. Anyway,' he went on, 'in the interests of fairness I must remind you that it's a little over five years since he last offered me a brief, and that could in no way be described as a family matter.'

'But earlier the same year,' said Sir Nicholas inexorably, 'he induced Jenny to visit an aunt of his in some village with an unlikely name –'

'Burton Cecil.'

'– where she very nearly got herself killed.'

Antony grimaced at the memory. 'I shouldn't have let her go if I'd realised what was going to happen,' he said. 'But that was a special case after all. This is quite an ordinary brief and shouldn't hold any surprises.'

'Yes, and you've had some experience of so-called ordinary briefs in Arkenshaw,' said Sir Nicholas devastatingly. 'The first time, if I recollect, there was some talk of hitting you over the head and dumping you in the canal. The second time you actually did land in the water –'

'My foot slipped,' said Antony apologetically.

'You were also involved in a car accident and a bomb was placed in your room at the hotel,' said Sir Nicholas, not to be diverted. 'The last time, I admit, you seem to have taken some reasonable precautions before it actually came to violence, but the record as a whole is not a good one.'

'But Uncle Nick,' Jenny protested, 'we've spent a few days with Chris and Star every summer now for ages, and nothing's ever happened.'

8

'That is quite a different matter. A holiday is one thing, but if Chris has called on Antony in this instance it can only mean that he wishes him to meddle in some affair or other. For instance . . . when exactly are you going to Arkenshaw, Antony?'

'I thought I'd take the train on Friday evening.'

'And when does the case come on?'

'Chris isn't quite sure. It might be the end of the following week.' He knew quite well that this answer was playing into his uncle's hands, but there was no way of avoiding the question.

'Exactly!' Sir Nicholas sounded triumphant. 'And that interval, I suppose, is intended to give you the opportunity of setting the whole town by the ears as you've done so often in the past.'

Antony grinned at him. 'Arkenshaw is quite an ordinary place, Uncle Nick, and Yorkshire isn't exclusively inhabited by thieves and cut-throats.'

'I suppose I must take your word for that.' His uncle's tone was grudging. 'I should like you to tell me, however, who your client is in this instance, and what he's charged with.'

'His name is Richard Willard, and he's an actor. He's charged with arranging for the murder of his wife.'

'Arranging?' asked Sir Nicholas sharply.

'Soliciting her murder, if we must be exact. Under Section 4 of the Offences against the Person Act of 1861,' he added unnecessarily.

'And was this intention successfully carried out?' asked his uncle, not at all grateful for the information.

'Apparently so. I don't know any details yet,' he added, in the hope of forestalling any further questions.

'One presumes, however, that the evidence must be of a circumstantial nature,' said Sir Nicholas thoughtfully.

'The question is,' said Vera, 'why does this particular case worry Chris and Star?'

'Willard is a friend of theirs.'

9

'You said,' Sir Nicholas reminded him accusingly, 'that it was "not altogether" a family matter. I think it's time for that explanation we asked for, if the approach to it has been sufficiently roundabout for you.'

'The woman, Mrs Willard, was shot down in the street. Unfortunately a police constable was also shot in attempting to prevent the murderer's escape. My old friend Constable Ryder to be exact.'

'Is he dead too?'

'I'm afraid so.'

'In that case I'm beginning to see Chris's difficulty,' said Sir Nicholas in a rather milder tone. 'That is . . . you say he believes in his friend's innocence?'

'I didn't say so, but it seems he does.'

Sir Nicholas turned to his wife. 'You've never met Chris Conway, my dear,' he said, 'though I've told you a good deal about Antony's dealings with him. His father-in-law is a member of the police force – an Inspector now if I remember rightly, Antony? – and Constable Ryder is one of his men.'

'So he blames his son-in-law for siding with the man he believes is the murderer,' said Vera, who was no more inclined than her husband to need any explanation to be carried to its conclusion.

'Precisely. Am I right, Antony?'

'Of course you are.'

'And Chris believes, rightly or wrongly, that you may be able to do something towards getting his client acquitted?'

'Yes.' Antony's hesitation before he spoke again was perfectly obvious to them all. 'But you see, Uncle Nick, it isn't enough just to get him off, we've got to persuade Inspector Duckett that it isn't merely insufficient evidence, or reasonable doubt, or anything like that.'

'Hence the invitation to meddle. Well, I see your point, Antony, you want to help your friend if you can. But what if it turns out that Inspector Duckett is right, and Chris is wrong?'

'The situation will be . . . difficult,' Maitland admitted.

'Unless, of course, Willard decides to plead Guilty,' he added more hopefully.

'I imagine that is not his intention, or Chris would not have called on you so urgently.'

'No, I don't suppose it is. If he insists he didn't do it the only thing will be to deal with the matter as I would with any other case until the verdict's in. After that –' he paused to smile at Jenny and then at Vera and then looked back at his uncle again '– how do you fancy me in the role of peacemaker?' he asked.

Surprisingly it was Jenny who answered this. 'Inspector Duckett's a very determined man,' she said.

'So he is, love. But he's also Star's father, and Star, in his eyes, can do no wrong. I know he chose that ghastly name himself,' he added, by way of explanation to Vera. 'It's nothing to do with Grandma Duckett's interest in astrology, of which I'm sure I've spoken to you. But I've always felt it indicated a certain poetic streak in him which you'd never otherwise suspect.'

Vera considered this. 'Far-fetched,' she commented.

'I don't know that I altogether agree with you. Anyway, the situation may be sticky at the moment but it won't last indefinitely,' he assured her with confidence. 'But you do see – even you must admit, Uncle Nick – that Chris is far too good a friend for me to let him down.'

'I see you're determined to have your own way about this,' said Sir Nicholas, rather unfairly returning to his original complaint, 'but there are two further questions I wish to ask you.' He paused there, glancing at Jenny, who smiled serenely back at him, but it was from Maitland that the interruption came.

'We've talked it over; Jenny quite agrees that I should go.'

'Jenny,' said Sir Nicholas dampeningly, 'has no more sense than you have.'

'The question you're hesitating about asking me,' said Antony, 'is, I suppose, who killed Willard's wife? The answer is, I don't know. But if it was a hit-man –'

11

Sir Nicholas shuddered. 'I always said no good would come of that trip you made to the United States,' he remarked. 'If by that vile phrase you mean a hired assassin –'

'If you prefer that way of putting it,' said Antony, not altogether hiding his amusement, or even attempting to hide it. 'What I was going to say was, if there's one thing that's certain in this uncertain world it's that he won't be in Arkenshaw any longer. And if he was, why should he wish to harm me? Even Jenny sees the logic in that.'

'Things that might have been put more tactfully,' said Vera, and turned her head to smile at Jenny. 'Think she has a very good understanding,' she added reprovingly.

'Don't disillusion me, Vera. Surely you realise that Jenny's illogical point of view in this intensely legal household is one of the things I value most about her.'

'Another being that she always lets you have your own way,' said Sir Nicholas drily. 'However, I'll admit the force of that argument.'

'I thought you would. What was the other question, Uncle Nick?' However much he might digress, Maitland could always be counted on to return to the subject in hand.

'Merely about this Richard Willard who you say is an actor. I don't seem to have heard of him.'

'I don't think he's made it to the West End yet. I think he's about Chris's age – somewhere in his mid-thirties anyway – so there's still time, but he seems to have plenty of work in the provinces and perhaps that satisfies him.'

'Have you asked Meg if she knows anything about him?'

'Not yet, but Jenny's asked her to lunch tomorrow, and unless my morning conferences last too long I'll come home for the meal. And – who knows? – if I ask Grandma Duckett to read my horoscope when I get to Arkenshaw I may be able to assure you without any further delay that there's nothing to worry about at all!'

II

Antony and Jenny Maitland had for many years had their own quarters on the two top floors of Sir Nicholas's house in Kempenfeldt Square. The fact that this had been originally a temporary measure had long since been forgotten: it was an arrangement that suited them all, particularly as Maitland was a member of his uncle's chambers in the Inner Temple, and many a legal battle had been fought either in the study downstairs, or round the fire in the Maitland's living room.

Sir Nicholas had married in 1971, at the end of the Trinity Term, Miss Vera Langhorne, barrister-at-law, but if anyone had thought to mention it it would have been generally agreed that this added to rather than detracted from the comfort of the household. His housekeeper, Mrs Stokes, had long been accustomed to getting her own way, but fortunately she had taken a fancy to Vera and humoured her, within reason. As for Gibbs the butler, who was something in the nature of a family heirloom, he was a disagreeable old man who would have been pensioned off years ago if his employer had had his way. But though his duties now were exactly what he wished to make them he enjoyed being a martyr and all attempts to persuade him of the benefits of retirement had failed. Nothing would ever make him into what Antony would have described as a little ray of sunshine, but at least he too approved of the newcomer, and since her arrival had given up a number of his more annoying habits, such as ignoring the house phone and insisting on stumping up two flights of stairs every time there was a visitor for Antony or Jenny, in the well-founded hope of making them feel guilty.

The Tuesday evening dinners with the Maitlands dated from the days of Sir Nicholas's bachelorhood, because Tuesday was sacred to Mrs Stokes's weekly visits to the cinema and he preferred Jenny's hospitality to the cold collation that had originally been his fare on those occasions.

Now, when he had closed the door behind their visitors, Maitland went back into the big living room and found Jenny restoring the decanters to their place of concealment and replacing them on the tray with the used glasses. The fire was dying but the room was still warm. 'Come and sit down a minute,' he requested.

'Uncle Nick's only carrying on about your going to Arkenshaw because he hates a case that takes either of you out of town,' said Jenny, correctly divining what was in his mind. But she left her task and came to join him.

'He made me wonder . . . do you really not mind my going, Jenny?'

'I shan't like your going away, I never do,' she told him. 'But even if it weren't for Chris you have to go where your job takes you, and there's absolutely no other reason for me to mind.'

'My dearest love, what a little liar you are,' said Antony, raising his left hand to rumple still further her brown-gold curls. 'You know if it upsets you I'd even tell Chris to go to the devil.'

'Everything you said to Uncle Nick was perfectly true . . . and logical,' said Jenny smiling at him.

He looked at her searchingly for a moment. 'If you're sure,' he said doubtfully.

'I am sure. But if you really want to upset me, Antony, you'll start acting on what you imagine my feelings to be.'

On the rare occasions when he could be brought to speak honestly of his own emotions Antony would admit that Jenny's peace of mind (serenity was the word he always used to himself) was one of the most important things in his life, something to cling to when the going got particularly rough. But now her grey eyes met his with their usual candour. 'Even if there were anything to worry about,' she assured him, 'it wouldn't make any difference so long as you told me.'

'Yes, love, it took me a long time to realise that, didn't it? And I have to admit, apart from wanting to help Chris, the small amount he told me about the case intrigued me.'

14

'Yes, I thought so.' She saw that he still wanted to talk and sat down again, patting the sofa beside her invitingly. After a momentary hesitation he joined her. 'It's funny to think,' Jenny went on, 'that a few months ago both Uncle Nick and Vera would have jumped at the chance of getting you out of town for a week or two, just to be out of Superintendent Briggs's way.'

'Yes, I know. That's one of the reasons he's carrying on so about this trip north – he has to have something to complain about – and Briggs's activities have kept him pretty well occupied in that direction for quite a number of years.' He leaned back and stretched out his long legs and looked at her, smiling. 'You were right all of you, and I was wrong,' he said reminiscently. 'I thought as long as I kept on the right side of the law nothing particularly bad could happen, I never dreamed Briggs would actually flip his lid and try and frame me.'

'Well, there's nothing more to worry about on that score,' said Jenny with satisfaction. 'Except perhaps,' she added with an impish look, 'that you may forget yourself and use that expression in front of Uncle Nick. He'd consider it another "vile phrase".'

'It's good for his soul,' Antony told her. 'What I wanted to tell you, love: I had lunch with Sykes today.'

'Why didn't you tell me before? He hadn't any – any axe to grind, had he?'

'No, just a bit of news. And I suppose it was force of habit that kept me quiet on the subject while Uncle Nick was here, he's always carried on so about my getting mixed up with the police. I'll tell him tomorrow if I remember.'

'What was the news?' asked Jenny with curiosity.

'He's been promoted and is now Detective-Superintendent Sykes.'

'Oh dear, I shall never remember that,' said Jenny.

'No love, I don't suppose you will. And I don't suppose he'll care one way or the other,' Antony assured her. 'Mayhew got his promotion too and is now Chief Inspector.

And they're getting a new Assistant Commissioner (Crime) at last. Sir Edwin's decided to retire, obviously feeling that he's had enough. And the way things are today I can't say that I blame him.'

'Who will the new man be?'

'Sykes doesn't know yet. The other bit of news is that Briggs has moved himself and Mrs Briggs to a cottage in the country. Sykes did tell me where, but I've forgotten again. Somewhere on the south coast.'

'I'm glad about that.'

'It doesn't make any difference to us, love, he was out of the CID in any case.'

'Yes, but . . . if someone is going to sit around hating you I'd rather he did it at a distance,' said Jenny. 'And now you'll say I'm being illogical again,' she added.

'Beautifully illogical, Jenny love,' said Antony with satisfaction. 'And since we've decided to take no notice of Uncle Nick prophesying doom over this expedition of mine, will you try to think of something I could take to Star? And something for young Tony, of course. He must be eight now, and as he seems to be of a practical turn of mind . . . well, you'll know the kind of thing.'

'If Meg has time I'll take her shopping with me tomorrow afternoon,' Jenny promised. 'And you'll give my love to them, of course, and to Grandma Duckett if you see her. I hope the Inspector won't be so cross he won't allow you to enter the house.'

'Grandma has a mind of her own, love, I don't think she'd stand for anything like that.'

Jenny smiled again. 'Yes, I know,' she said, 'and if I were really worried about your going to Arkenshaw again the thought of her would reassure me. If anybody is, I'd say she's capable of keeping you in order.'

III

Sir Nicholas and Vera had gone straight down to the study. It had always been Sir Nicholas's favourite room and this was fortunately a feeling which Vera seemed to share. Not that she had much choice, since she had, at Antony's suggestion and with her husband's connivance, turned the big drawing room into a music room to house the expensive stereo equipment which had been her one extravagance before her marriage. Sir Nicholas, who had finished the book he was reading the previous night, was looking along the shelves for another.

'Tell you something,' said Vera to his back, 'that nephew of yours –'

'Ours, my dear,' Sir Nicholas corrected her gently, not turning round.

'What's the difference?'

'I decline to take full responsibility for Antony, since I am bound to point out that my influence over him has been greatly diminished since you generally appear to take his part.' He took down a book and turned with it in his hands to smile at her.

'From what you've told me,' said Vera, no whit abashed, 'always inclined to go his own way. Don't think you'd want it otherwise,' she added acutely.

'You may be right, my dear,' Sir Nicholas agreed meekly.

'What I was going to say' – nobody had yet succeeded in diverting Vera from a point she wished to make – 'is that I think Antony was more worried than he ever admitted about that man Briggs.'

'I've always found him reasonably truthful,' said Sir Nicholas thoughtfully.

'Yes, of course. Might have been his subconscious,' said Vera.

Her husband, who was well used to her elliptical way of speaking, gave that his consideration. 'I expect you're right,' he said. He was a tall man, as tall as his nephew though of a very different type, but it sometimes happened that an onlooker might be startled by an elusive resemblance between them, which could be one of expression only considering the difference in their appearance. Sir Nicholas was more heavily built and his hair was so fair that any grey there might have been in it was successfully concealed. He had an air of unconscious authority about him, which contrasted with Maitland's more casual manner, and the press had a habit of referring to him – without too much exaggeration – as handsome, a fact which had the worst effect on his always uncertain temper if it came to his attention. Jenny, since her marriage, and now Jenny and Vera between them, always did their best to suppress the offending articles, though not always with success. 'I have to admit, my dear,' said Sir Nicholas now, 'that the satisfactory conclusion of that particular problem has been a great relief to me, as I'm sure it has to you and Jenny. Like you, I have detected recently a certain relaxation in Antony's manner, as though he had been under a strain which has now been removed. I should not, however, wish to encourage him unduly in this light-heartedness.'

Vera nodded wisely and the last of the pins which were supposed to hold her old-fashioned bun in place dropped silently to the floor. She had a mass of dark hair, flecked with grey now but as thick and heavy as when she had been younger. Since her marriage a clever couturier had achieved a certain sense of style in the loose-fitting garments she preferred, and they were certainly more colourful than once they had been, but nothing, thought her husband eyeing her affectionately, was ever going to change the essential Vera. 'Know exactly what you mean,' she told him now, vehemently. 'Never know what he'll be up to next!'

Wednesday, 29th January

The conference the next morning was with Geoffrey Horton – a solicitor who had often briefed Maitland in the past and by now was an old friend – and his client, a surly-looking youth who was part of a group charged with unlawful assembly but now out on bail. There was no real urgency about it, as it seemed unlikely that the case would be heard much before the Easter recess, and as the only contribution their client had to make was to reiterate his statement that, 'We didn't mean no harm,' the matter didn't detain them long. Geoffrey suggested lunch when they were alone again, but Maitland explained his mission, adding however, 'You know Jenny, she always prepares enough to feed an army. Why don't you join us?' But Geoffrey had work awaiting him and had been thinking in terms of a quick glass of beer and a sandwich, and declined the invitation.

Meg and Roger Farrell were the Maitlands' closest friends. Roger might be considered a paradox, being by occupation a stockbroker, but by inclination a man of action. A good man to have with you in a tight corner, as Maitland knew well enough. Meg was better known as Margaret Hamilton, and because her professional engagements were almost continuous Antony at least didn't see as much of her as he did of Roger, who was a frequent visitor to Kempenfeldt Square in the evenings when his wife was at the theatre. Meg was not very tall,

19

and slightly built, and unless the part she was playing called for some other style she wore her long, dark hair plaited and pinned neatly round her head. Since she first came to London to play Lady Macbeth she had acquired an air of elegance and certain affectations which always amused Maitland, remembering as he did the unsophisticated girl they had first known. Though she had by no means always stuck to Shakespeare she had only recently tried her hand at something in a lighter vein. But that play, in spite of its success, had come off last year, and now she was deep in rehearsals for *Othello*.

As Gibbs hadn't been expecting either his employer or his employer's nephew home that lunchtime he was absent from the hall when Maitland let himself in. He appeared, however, before Antony had reached the half-landing, and replied rather repressively to his greeting. 'Mrs Farrell arrived quite half an hour ago, Mr Maitland,' he added, with the unspoken implication that if you were expecting her to lunch you should have been here before her. But Maitland was too used to his ways for that to worry him; only if he was particularly tired or if his shoulder was more painful than usual – often a simultaneous occurrence – might the old man's attitude prove an irritation. On this occasion he acknowledged the information briefly, thinking only that it was good to have the time, and a ready-made excuse, to allow him to come home at this hour.

Jenny was drinking a gin and tonic and had persuaded Meg to a small glass of her favourite Dubonnet. Antony greeted them, provided himself with scotch and grinned as he turned to find Meg's eye disapprovingly on him. 'I'm not in court today,' he said, answering her unspoken comment. 'And if you two are going to set me a bad example –'

'I shan't be able to have a drink tonight, darling,'

20

said Meg, rather as though she were afraid that he might think she was becoming an alcoholic, 'because of the dress rehearsal.'

'Good lord, I didn't know you'd got on as far as that. In that case, Meg, you don't want to be bothered with my questions. Let's just relax and enjoy ourselves.'

'He says that almost as if he meant it,' said Meg, turning to Jenny. 'Don't worry, darling, you won't be asking me much when you realise how little I know about this Richard Willard of yours. Besides, you know I never gossip.'

'But you do know him?'

'I know *of* him,' said Meg precisely. 'Jon knew him, years ago when they were playing together in Bradford or somewhere like that.' (Jon Kellaway was playing Othello to her Desdemona.)

'In that case . . . look here, Meg, it isn't gossiping. He needs my help and I need yours. It's bound to be a good thing all round if I know something of him before I get to Arkenshaw.'

'Well, I don't know anything nasty about him, darling,' said Meg, 'so from that point of view I suppose it wouldn't matter. Jenny says he's murdered his wife.'

'I said he was accused of arranging for her murder,' Jenny protested. 'Antony and Uncle Nick and Vera had a different way of putting it, but that's what they meant. And you know, Meg, being accused isn't at all the same thing as having done it.'

'Yes, I know, darling.' If anyone in this world could get round Meg, even when her Presbyterian upbringing was rearing its head, it was Jenny. 'But really . . . Jenny says the solicitor who's briefing you is a friend of Richard Willard, so I'm sure he can tell you far more than I can.'

'They're friends,' said Maitland stressing the word. 'That means Chris Conway's judgement is likely to be prejudiced . . . don't you think?'

21

'Yes, I suppose so. But I do think, darling,' said Meg reprovingly, 'that you ought to be capable of making up your own mind when you see him.'

Maitland grinned at that. He was a man whose sense of humour was never very far beneath the surface, even, unfortunately, when the occasion demanded a strict and sober attendance to duty. He was still on his feet, one shoulder propped against the high mantel, and his glass standing by the clock. 'You know me, Meg,' he said, 'I'm always plagued by doubts. The only thing I'm sure about is that I can't take a chance on condemning someone just on my own opinion. But I'm not asking you to tell me whether Willard is innocent or guilty, only to give me a little background information about him.'

Meg looked up at him and returned his smile. 'You'll be disappointed,' she warned him.

'Disappoint me then.'

'Well, of course, when he was arrested everyone in the company was interested, because of his being a member of the profession. And then Jon told me he'd known him about fifteen years ago, perhaps not as much as that. But he didn't say anything to the others because I think he's still a little sensitive about what nearly happened to him and didn't want to listen to a lot of uninformed speculation.'

Maitland ignored this reference to a case in which he had himself been involved at Meg's instigation. 'Fifteen years,' he said thoughtfully. 'That must have been right at the beginning of Willard's career.'

'It may not have been quite as much as that. I'll tell you how you'll know; it was the year that Richard Willard got married.'

'I don't know when that was, but I expect Chris will. Are you telling me he married young?'

'Well, he must have, mustn't he, I mean he's years younger than Jon? And I remember now, it was Arkenshaw they were playing, not Bradford. But it's all

22

the same, isn't it?'

'Not exactly. Didn't Jenny tell you it was the Crown Court at Arkenshaw I'm going to, where Willard will be tried?'

'If she did, darling, I can't have been listening. But that makes sense, because that was where he met . . . I think the girl's name was Laura. Jon says she was a local girl, so I daresay that's where they settled. You can live out of suitcases for just so long, but you do need a permanent base, especially if there's a baby coming.'

'Was that why they were married?'

'Darling, how would I know?'

'Well, did this play – whatever it was – in Arkenshaw have a long run?'

'They were both in the repertory theatre there for a whole winter as far as I remember. Jon and Richard Willard, I mean. It was just a few years before Jon got his chance in *A Kind of Praise.*'

'Tell me what Jon had to say about Richard Willard.'

'He liked him, I think. I'm not absolutely sure, darling, whether it was because he was a good actor or whether it was for himself. But being so young he was given the part of a teenager, a pretty objectionable teenager Jon said, and he did it very well. There was nobody else in the company who was even as young as he really was, so I expect that's why he made friends outside. Anyway he'd met – I'm sure it was Laura – before Christmas, because he brought her with him to the company's Christmas party.'

'And what about her?'

'If you mean what did Jon say about her, not very much. She was a very young girl, and he doesn't remember a great deal about her. Except that she was pretty, and that he got the impression the two of them were very much in love. They were married early in the new year, and before the season ended – I think that was in April or the beginning of May but I don't suppose it matters – Richard was boasting there was a baby coming. Jon left the company then, but as far as he remembers Richard was going back the following year. But they'd nothing in common of course, with the difference in ages, so that was the last they saw of each other. Knowing the name Jon's noticed it from time to time in the papers, and he got the impression that Richard was doing quite well for himself, without becoming one of the top people. He's been travelling about a good deal, but unless there were more children that wouldn't matter so much when the baby got a bit older. Jon can't understand the charge –'

'It's very clear.'

'I don't mean the legal jargon. If Richard Willard arranged for murder to be done it's the same as doing it himself really, isn't it? But Jon says he was sure the marriage was one that was going to last.'

'If they were both very young –' He broke off, looking at Jenny. 'I shouldn't be the one to say that, should I, love? But it does sometimes happen that people grow apart.'

'Sometimes,' Jenny agreed, smiling at him.

He turned back to Meg. 'Does Willard have any family?'

'No relations,' said Meg, 'except his wife, of course, and whatever the baby turned out to be. And any more children that may have come along.'

'I didn't mean that exactly, I meant before his marriage.'

'None as far as Jon knew.'

'And Mrs Willard?'

'Jon only met her that once, and then again at the wedding. He says there were crowds of people on her side of the church, but he doesn't know which ones were related to her.' Meg searched her mind for a moment. 'Her name was Hargreaves,' she added helpfully.

'So she was a local girl, but he wasn't from

Arkenshaw. I wonder how it comes about that he's a friend of Chris's.'

'If they made their home in Arkenshaw –' said Jenny, but did not elaborate on the point. 'And you know, Antony, about a possible motive, it *is* a difficult profession.'

'Not a bit of it, darling.' Meg was positive. 'Look at Roger and me. If you go about it the right way –'

She didn't attempt to complete the thought, but Antony, out of his affection for both the Farrells, mentally did so for her, And if you have a husband as forbearing as Roger is. But he had spoken his mind to her on that subject years ago, as he had done to Roger before they were married, and as, in spite of all Meg's vagaries, there was no doubt about their happiness, there was no need for him to repeat himself.

As he was leaving to go back to chambers Meg was inclined to be apologetic. 'I hope you weren't expecting any startling disclosures, darling,' she said. 'I expect you'll find she met someone else and it was just a case of jealousy.'

Antony and Jenny exchanged a look and spoke almost simultaneously. 'We don't know yet that he did anything wrong,' said Jenny, and, 'Roger said we'd have to put up with you playing Desdemona all over the place,' said Antony gloomily.

'You'll have to see me doing it in earnest tomorrow night,' Meg reminded him. 'I know you've forgotten but you promised to come to the opening.'

'I haven't forgotten that, just how much of the month was gone. So we'll see you after the show, Meg, and thank you for putting your scruples on one side for a moment.'

'Not to much purpose, I'm afraid.'

'You never can tell,' said Maitland sententiously, 'what may turn out to be useful.' But privately he agreed with her.

Friday, 31st January

The opening night had been a triumph, as Antony had expected. He knew Jon Kellaway for a fine actor, and he was never in any doubt about Meg being able to carry off any role she chose. But the aftermath had gone on too long for his taste, and he was already tired when he left chambers the following evening to catch the train from King's Cross to Arkenshaw. The journey should have been restful, but for some reason his mind was working all the time at full stretch.

He hadn't much to go on in regard to the matter in which he was about to embroil himself, but judging from Chris's almost desperate tone on the telephone the situation between him and his father-in-law might be more serious than Maitland had tried to make out when talking to his family. In addition, some of the more magniloquent lines from the play the previous evening kept repeating themselves over and over in his head. There was no doubt that Jon Kellaway, unlikely a choice as he might seem, had made a splendid Othello; while as for Meg . . . he had a private theory that Meg was capable of playing any part, however difficult, though perhaps it wouldn't be good for her soul to tell her so. Desdemona's lines would prove no difficulty to an experienced actress, but that Meg should succeed in subduing her forthright nature to such an extent as to make the character believable was wonder enough in itself; that she should at the same time achieve the paradox of dominating the action equally with the more outspoken Othello was well nigh a miracle.

It was about nine-thirty when he finally arrived in Arkenshaw, and as he got out of the train he was immediately conscious of the cold, and the chilly wind that swept up the platform. It must have been nearly five years since he had accomplished the journey by train and alone; though summer visits, with Jenny driving him over from their friend Bill's farm, which was further up Thorburndale, were a very different matter. But, as he had expected, when he reached the barrier and surrendered his ticket he found that Chris Conway, his friend now of many years standing and, on this occasion, his instructing solicitor, was among those waiting to greet the travellers. Chris was punctilious in these matters, and his faintly worried look was by now so familiar that it caused Antony no additional disquiet.

Conway possessed himself firmly of Maitland's suitcase, which he had been carrying along clumsily with his briefcase in his left hand – his right arm, owing to the injury to his shoulder (as all his friends knew but few dared mention), being useless for tasks like that. Conway asked as soon as greetings had been exchanged, 'Do you want to go straight to the hotel, or will you come home with me first?'

'Home, if it isn't too much trouble.'

'Of course it isn't, Star's been expecting us. No, this way,' he added, as Maitland turned automatically towards Chris's usual parking place in what should have been a stand for taxis only. 'They're a bit more fussy about these things nowadays, so I park down here now . . . legally.'

'I suppose that means you got a ticket once.'

'Yes, and you can't let that sort of thing become a habit,' said Chris, heaving the suitcase into the boot and slamming the lid. He was a little shorter than Maitland, with grey eyes and regular features, and a fair complexion that probably meant his rather unruly brown hair had been a reddish shade when he was younger. 'Of course, if you'd rather go out to the prison –' he went on, grinning, and didn't attempt to complete the sentence.

Nor did Antony make the obvious retort, that the offer

27

couldn't in any case have been implemented at that time of night. 'You'll never let me forget that will you?' he asked amiably, getting into the car. The first time they had met he had disconcerted Chris by demanding to see his client immediately; a fact which he sometimes regretted as the solicitor had a long memory and was on occasion inclined to forestall what he thought would be counsel's demand for action, usually at a time when Maitland wanted nothing better than to relax with a drink.

Outside the station all was familiar. Perhaps after all Arkenshaw really looked its best after darkness had fallen, though the cold of the winter's night allowed Antony to feel his usual pang of sympathy for the lightly draped nymphs who guarded the fountain in the centre of the square. They had turned right out of the station into Swinegate, but the way to Ingleton Crescent, where the Conways lived, was familiar by now, and Maitland was more interested in his companion than in the passing scene. Chris was the most cautious driver he knew, and the fact that he had to accomplish a right turn to get into his own street still seemed a cause for some anxiety, even though there were traffic lights guarding the intersection. But the turn into the terrace of substantial grey stone houses was accomplished in safety.

Number eleven was the sixth house on the left from the corner. 'We're almost the only private house left along here,' said Chris as he pulled up, 'which makes parking easier at this time of night.' Even as he spoke the front door opened, and by the time they had got out of the car Star Conway was halfway down the steps to meet them.

As he might have expected, her greeting, after she had embraced him warmly, was strictly practical. 'Have you had anything to eat?' she asked.

'Yes, I ate on the train.'

'Then come in out of the cold, and Chris shall get you a drink.' Maitland didn't have to look at his friend to know that his expression had lightened at the sight of his wife. Which was nothing to be surprised at, even if you went by no

28

more than appearances. Star was a small woman, very much Meg's build in fact, but with a cloud of dark hair, hazel eyes, and no affectations at all. Her attraction lay in the warm friendliness of her manner, so that – though he'd rather have been going home to Kempenfeldt Square – her greeting made this certainly the next best thing.

Surprisingly, Star bustled him into the living room before he had had time to shrug his way out of his overcoat. 'I had a job getting young Tony to bed,' she confided, 'and if he hears us he'll be down again. So just leave your coats on the chair by the door and come to the fire. You must be starved.' Which, as Maitland knew well enough, was a comment on the coldness of the night, not on the adequacy or otherwise of the meal British Rail had provided.

'I've got a small gift for my namesake, it's in my suitcase in the car,' he told her.

'And it can stay there for tonight,' said Star decidedly. 'I'm not risking another tussle with him, and I'm sure you two want to talk business.'

Antony smiled at her, amused at this echo of Chris's own approach to him when they were working together. 'I suppose we ought to,' he admitted. 'Though I'd much rather just sit quietly and hear your news.'

Chris was investigating a corner cupboard. 'Scotch or brandy?' he asked over his shoulder.

'Brandy, please, but not if I'm going to be drinking alone.'

'No, we'll join you. At least, I expect you'll have a *crème de menthe*, Star?' He poured the drinks and served them, and came to sit down near the fire. 'The thing is,' he said, 'that our news and the matter I brought you here on are all mixed up together at the moment. So I'd like to get it off my chest, and you won't mind Star staying. She knows all about it anyway, because Richard talked to both of us before he was arrested.'

'I shouldn't mind anyway. You've sat in on our conferences at Kempenfeldt Square often enough when you've been in town, Chris. In any case, so far as I've been

29

able to observe, all Yorkshire women have a built-in sense of discretion,' he added, smiling.

'You're thinking of Grandma Duckett and her objection to what she calls scurrilous talk,' said Chris.

'Yes, how is she?'

It was Star who answered. 'No good will come of it,' she said, shaking her head in a despondent way, and then immediately smiling at Antony to show that this was merely a quotation.

'I suppose your friend was born under the wrong sign of the Zodiac,' said Antony seriously.

'Yes, of course. Scorpio,' said Chris, rather as though it were an imprecation.

'I thought it was Pisces people like you who were particularly abhorrent to her.'

'Scorpio seems to be just as bad. Unreliable,' said Chris, 'and the planet Mercury being dominant just makes matters worse.'

'I see. Well, I expect she'll tell me all that herself, or . . . we're not forbidden in the house, are we?'

'Nothing like that but . . . I think I'd better begin at the beginning,' said Chris. 'The question is, what is the beginning?'

'Seven years ago,' Star suggested. 'When Richard came to your office at the time he and Laura were separating.'

'I didn't know . . . were they divorced?' Maitland asked.

'No.'

'A legal separation then?'

'Not that either. Though that was why he came to see me. He wanted to know if there would be any advantage in taking that course, but when he described the situation to me I had to tell him he'd just be wasting his money. Only . . . there are some people you take to instinctively, and I asked him to dinner here one night, and Star liked him too, and after that we've seen him whenever he's in town.'

Maitland was thinking inevitably that an instinctive liking was not always the best basis for trust. When he and

Chris had first met, for instance, it had taken the solicitor some time to get used to his ways. But this didn't seem to be the time to bring that up. 'And what was the situation?' he asked.

'I told you Richard is an actor, and a good one too, I believe. We've seen plays he's been in, of course, but I wouldn't say either of us is qualified to judge. Anyway, he's very rarely out of work, even though he's never achieved the West End. I'm not even sure that he wants to.'

'Come now, I thought that was the goal of everybody connected with the stage.'

'Well . . . perhaps. I'm not quoting him, you know, only giving you an impression, and from what he told me, even at that first meeting, his financial affairs are quite stable.'

'You were telling me the situation in which he and his wife found themselves which led to his consulting you,' said Antony patiently.

'Yes, of course. He isn't a local chap, and he met Laura when he was playing in the repertory company here one winter. They fell in love and married pretty quickly, and before the season was over she knew she was pregnant and they decided they ought to have a proper home to provide some sort of stability for the baby, who turned out to be a boy. Jamie. And as Laura was a local girl, she wanted that home to be here.'

'And Willard agreed?'

'Yes, it seemed quite a good choice even apart from her having some of her family close by. Wherever they went he'd have to be away a good deal, but Arkenshaw is pretty central and it meant that if he picked his jobs carefully he could get home quite often. As you know an actor's life isn't really the best basis for marriage; continual separations and all that sort of thing. They never quarrelled, he was emphatic about that, but Laura quite soon got tired of having him so often away. He tried to persuade her that they could afford to keep the house as a place to come back to when he was resting, and, at least until Jamie was ready for school, they could

31

both accompany him. Then later there'd be boarding school, he was sure things could be worked out somehow. I don't know whether he was right about that, but anyway Laura wouldn't agree. So they just went on as they were for the time being.'

'This, I take it, is what he told you on that first occasion when he came to your office.'

'Yes, that's right.'

'Did you ever meet Laura?'

'I went to see her at that time, because I wanted to make sure; not that Richard was telling the truth, because I was sure he was as he saw it, but whether he was completely right about her attitude.'

'Which was?'

'She was tired of the position and wanted to separate, but she'd no desire to marry again, and no animosity towards Richard. She wouldn't stop him seeing Jamie whenever he had the chance, which I think by then was the thing that mattered most to him. So he made arrangements for a quite generous allowance for the two of them, and I had to advise him that there was no need for further action unless either of them changed their minds about re-marrying.'

'So how have things gone on since then?'

'I think Richard has deliberately arranged his work so as not to be too far away. He might have stayed with the repertory here if he hadn't had to compete for every leading part with a local man who was already with the company before he joined it. He's been in Rothershaw for the last few years, during the winter season that is, and in the summer he'd be working in one or other of the coastal towns, but of course in the good weather that didn't make any difficulty. He'd drive over most Sunday mornings and take Jamie out for the day. At first, of course, he had to take the boy home fairly early, and that's how he got into the habit of coming to dinner with us, and after a while we asked him to stay over instead of going to the hotel. Then he could drive back to Rothershaw, or wherever he was playing, on the Monday morning. As Jamie grew older he was able to stay out later, and sometimes he'd come here with his father or else have an early dinner with him in town.'

'Did Jamie seem to feel any resentment towards his father for leaving them?'

'No, none at all.'

'They always seemed on very good terms,' Star put in. 'Completely at ease with each other. Anyway, as Chris said, it was Laura who wanted the separation.'

'I don't suppose the boy would know that.'

'No, Richard said they told him they'd both agreed that it would be better for them to live apart,' said Chris. 'But I think you're wondering whether Laura ever tried to influence Jamie's opinion of his father. I can only say there was no sign at all that she ever did so, and she certainly never tried to prevent them from seeing each other.'

'And how did the separation work on your friend Willard's feelings?'

'That's hard to answer. I can honestly say I've never heard him say a word against Laura –'

'That's perfectly true,' Star interrupted him, 'but I'm quite sure his affection for her had gradually faded, not to dislike exactly but certainly to indifference.' She paused, looking from one of the two men to the other. 'Well, I know from experience that Antony should know the very worst that can be said,' she added defiantly; so that Maitland had a sudden vision of the girl he had first met ten years ago when he was defending her father on a charge of wrongful arrest, and she had annoyed the then Sergeant Duckett by insisting that certain matters he considered irrelevant should be brought to his counsel's notice. It wasn't everybody, he thought, looking at her affectionately, who would realise that loyalty must sometimes take strange forms, or who would have the courage to act on that realisation. But Star was loyal to the core, and there was no doubt about her courage.

'You like Richard Willard, Star?' he asked.

'Of course I do!'

'You feel you can trust him?' he insisted.

'Yes, in everything,' she told him firmly.

'It has been said that murder is the one crime that anybody might commit, given sufficient provocation.'

'Yes, but not in this way. Not in cold calculation, getting someone else to do the job for you. Richard could never have done that.'

Chris had been looking from one to the other of them with some amusement. 'I gather, Antony, that you're more willing to accept Star's opinion than mine,' he said. 'But, still, I may as well add my twopenn'orth. I agree with her completely about that.'

'I'd already gathered as much,' said Maitland noncommittally. 'Well, you've described the position between Willard and his wife very clearly, but was it still exactly the same at the time of her death? Had there been any change that would give him a motive for killing her?'

'I'm afraid there had,' said Chris reluctantly. 'Laura had changed her mind about wanting to marry again.'

'From what Star told me that wouldn't have made him jealous.'

'No, nothing like that. If it had been a matter of granting her a divorce, I'm sure he'd have done it like a shot.'

'What was the trouble then?'

'The man concerned.'

'But if his feeling towards her was one of indifference, why should he care who she married?'

'It wasn't Laura's prospective husband he objected to, but Jamie's prospective stepfather.'

'I see,' said Maitland slowly. Or do I? he wondered.

'You're not explaining this at all well,' said Star. 'You see, Antony, the man was a member of one of those hellfire religions –'

'The Levellers,' said Chris. 'Don't you remember, Antony, we came across them when we were defending Tommy Ridealgh?'

'How could I forget? They don't disapprove of divorce

then?' Antony replied.

'Apparently not. The trouble is they *do* disapprove of actors, and Eardley had said quite definitely that once he and Laura were married the visits from Richard must stop.'

'Would Laura have gone along with that?'

'From what Richard told me she was completely besotted, completely under Eardley's influence.'

'What's his full name?'

'Lionel Eardley.'

'Could he have got away with it? With stopping Jamie from seeing his father, I mean.'

'It would have meant that the divorce suit, instead of being amicable on both sides, would have turned into a rather unpleasant custody battle. And Eardley – he's a slimy creature if ever there was one – had discovered irregularities in Richard's life, as he called them.'

'What irregularities?'

'I didn't know any of this until Richard consulted me professionally about the matter,' said Chris. 'Not that I was naïve enough to think that he'd been living like a monk all these years, but what seems to have happened is that he formed what he called a lasting relationship with another member of the Rothershaw Repertory, a girl called Mary Norton. Apparently they'd been living together for three years now, both working in the winter, and Mary going wherever Richard's job took him during the summer months. I got the impression that neither of them cared for casual affairs, but they were both used to that kind of nomadic life so the arrangement suited them very well.'

'Then, why the hell didn't they regularise the position?'

'I asked Richard that, of course. He said he didn't know how Laura would take the idea of his marrying again. He'd have had to tell her to explain why he wanted a divorce, and he was afraid that if she took a dislike to Mary she'd stop him seeing Jamie as often as he'd been in the habit of doing. As I expect you've gathered, that would have been a pretty bad blow for him.'

'Heartbreaking,' said Star. And added, when the two men turned to look at her, 'Put yourself in his place, Chris, suppose it was Tony.'

'Yes, but we're not separated,' Chris objected. 'And if you do try to turn me out, my girl, I warn you I'm not going quietly.'

Maitland had been following his own train of thought. 'Do you think Laura would have done that?' he asked. 'That it should even have occurred to your friend gives me rather an odd idea of her.'

'At that time I'd have said quite definitely, no. If I'd known about Richard's relationship with Mary, I mean. I only met Laura the once, you understand, but she seemed a very reasonable sort and this question of Lionel Eardley hadn't arisen at that point. Besides there was the allowance Richard made her. I told you it was a generous one, the court might well have made a smaller alimony order, and if she'd turned awkward Richard might well have tried for that. I pointed all this out to him when he finally told me, but he said he hadn't thought it was worth risking it. He said he and Mary regarded themselves as married, and that had been good enough for them both.'

'And the position now? You talked about a custody battle, but after all Jamie had been living with his mother all these years.'

'Yes, I suppose I wasn't being quite accurate. Much as he'd have liked to, Richard knew there was no question of his having Jamie with him all the time.'

'But could Eardley and Laura have stopped him seeing the boy altogether? You know more about these things than I do, Chris; every time the question of divorce comes up in one of my cases I have to look the Rules up all over again.'

'Well, Laura is – was – Jamie's mother, and as far as I know had been leading a completely blameless life. And nobody could suppose for a moment that her relationship with Eardley would have led either of them from the straight and narrow; whatever her feelings he'd never have countenanced such a thing. But once Richard's *affaire* with Mary Norton was dragged into the open, there's no saying how things might have gone. I don't think either of them would have minded very much, in their profession it would hardly have been regarded as a scandal, but if they got a rather strait-laced judge ... you know yourself, Antony, the question of adultery can often cloud the issue in far more serious cases, and if Laura's counsel, prompted by Eardley, had talked convincingly enough about loose-living members of the acting profession, I think the best Richard could have hoped for would be visiting rights that were very drastically reduced.'

'I see. When did all this arise, and had he talked to Laura about it?'

'We first heard what was happening when he visited us in mid-December. Apparently Laura had told him that she wanted to get married a fortnight before, and of course his first instinct was to say, "All right then, let's get on with it." Then she told him about Eardley –'

'Wait a bit! Had Richard ever met this man?'

'Not then. But Laura explained that he was a very religious man, with no time at all for members of the acting profession, and that there'd have to be some change in the arrangements for him to see Jamie. It wasn't only his being on the stage; Lionel had told her about Mary. I gather they had a bit of a fight about it, but Richard didn't take it as seriously at that stage as he did later. He realised that Laura was in a state of mind to do whatever Eardley suggested, but he didn't think that they'd press the matter so hard in court that there'd be any question of changing the present arrangements. It was only the following week, when Laura ... well, I can only say she confronted him with Eardley, and the man – according to Richard – fairly spat out the accusation about Mary Norton. And followed it up with a tirade about the wickedness of stage performances in general and the people who took part in them in particular. At that stage Richard, not unnaturally, began to take the matter

37

seriously. I realised, we both did, that there was something up, something worrying him, but it wasn't until the next weekend that he confided in us.'

'And asked your advice?'

'Yes, and I told him very much what I've said to you, now. At his request I went to see Eardley and found him even more bigotted and spiteful than Richard had said.'

'Chris said he was a horrible man,' said Star. 'In fact, I'm only surprised he'd have anything to do with Laura because she'd once been married to an actor.'

'If I remember what we learned about the Levellers rightly,' said Antony slowly, 'he'd regard her as – what was the phrase the minister used, Chris? – a brand to be saved from the burning. As long as she repented of her past indiscretions and led what he considered was a good life in the future, everything would be all right. Anyway, Chris, do I gather that your visit didn't achieve anything?'

'On the contrary, it may have made matters worse. In any event matters rested there, and on my advice Richard didn't try to see Jamie over the holiday though I can tell you we had a pretty good argument about that. Only it seemed to me that the less unpleasantness there was about the matter before the divorce action came to court the better, and I hoped Laura's lawyer would be in touch with me so that things could be arranged with as little fuss as possible. But instead of that Richard phoned to say he'd been stuck with a summons alleging adultery with Mary Norton, and I think at that point we both realised it was to be nothing short of open war.'

'What did you do?'

'There was nothing much we could do. Richard came up to spend the night on the twenty-ninth of December, bringing Mary with him, and I got John Bushey round to go into the matter thoroughly because I thought he'd be as good as anyone else to represent him in court. There was just one hopeful thing. I don't know what Mary Norton's like on the stage, but in herself she's a very quiet personality, I think

38

she'd have been almost certain to make a good impression.'

'If they didn't think she was putting on an act for the occasion, as she'd be quite capable of doing, I suppose, all things considered.'

'Yes, John pointed that out, but not until I was talking to him later on about the matter. The less self-conscious Mary felt about things the better.'

'I gather you didn't think there was any pretence about her attitude.'

'No, I didn't,' said Chris, and almost simultaneously Star said emphatically,

'She's a really nice person.'

Antony turned to smile at her, but his next question was divided impartially between them. 'Was she very upset by the impending divorce action?'

It was Star who answered him. 'Yes, she was. Well, anyone would have been, wouldn't they? But I think . . . I do honestly think, Antony, that Chris was right and she was more upset for Richard's sake than for her own. About the possibility of his having to see less of Jamie, rather than about the scandal.'

'I'm a bit at a loss about the course of events since then,' Antony admitted. 'You didn't phone me till last Sunday —'

'That was the day Richard was arrested. And I know I didn't have time to send you a brief, but it's all ready now so I can give you the papers before you leave this evening.'

'That's not what's worrying me. You said the case might come on within a week from now.'

'Oh, you mean it seems rather soon. Well, you know Arkenshaw, Antony, we only have an assize at all – or rather had, until it became the Crown Court – because it was one of the oldest in the country. It's even been known, though I admit not very recently, for the town to have to give the judge a pair of white gloves because there were no cases for him to hear. So Richard's case will be the last to be heard on the winter list.'

'You could apply for an adjournment.'

'If you think it would help, I will, but unless there's anything to be gained I don't see the point of prolonging the agony for another three or four months at least. And if you're going to talk about a change of venue, the case has aroused some very strong feelings in the neighbourhood, but I can't say they're all on one side or the other. Laura was well-liked but she lived very quietly, and once it was known she wanted to marry a member of what I believe you once called a dotty sect, Antony, some of the sympathy evaporated.'

'That doesn't sound very reasonable.'

'Maybe not, but it's true all the same. And similarly the people who think that being an actor is synonymous with being immoral are pretty well evenly balanced with the people who think it's a glamorous profession. So you see —'

'I see you're giving me just a week to work a miracle,' said Antony drily. 'So I think perhaps the next thing is for you to tell me about the murder.'

'There was never any mystery about who actually shot Laura, only why he should have done so,' said Chris. 'A man called Edwin Porson, and as Sir Nicholas isn't here I'll tell you he's known to the police as a hit man' – Antony smiled, remembering his uncle's reaction to the phrase – 'though they've never been able to bring anything home to him before. This is the first time he's actually been seen in action.'

'That brings us, I suppose, to Constable Ryder.'

'Poor Jim,' said Star. 'It was a terrible thing to happen and I don't wonder that Dad's furious about it. But you're not really beginning at the beginning, Chris. He was known to be here before anyone knew what he was going to do.'

'You're quite right, that's where I should have started. He arrived in Arkenshaw on December the twelfth. The CID had tipped the local chaps off that, quite by chance, he'd been seen boarding a train at King's Cross, and inquiries had turned up the fact that this was where he had booked to. Of course, that might have been a blind, he might quite easily have got off in Leeds, the train was an express up to that point. Still, the detective branch thought they'd better make sure, and they sent somebody down to meet the train.'

'How – ?'

'He isn't difficult to recognise,' said Chris, ignoring the interruption. 'He has a scar all down the right side of his face. And he did actually come here, looking as respectable as you please, and put up at the Midland Hotel. Obviously there was some reason for him being here, and I don't think I'd be exaggerating if I said his presence made the local chaps a trifle nervous.'

'What's his background?'

'You of all people won't be under the impression that all gangland activity in London stopped when the Kray twins went to gaol. I expect the scar is a relic of some sort of gang warfare. The bunch that Porson runs with are mixed up in every crime in the calendar, as far as I can gather, but he was apparently their specialist in assassination when somebody who was a crack shot was needed. He's said to be utterly ruthless, and also very, very careful.'

'Just the sort of chap to put the cat among the pigeons in a place like this,' Maitland commented.

'You may well say so. The local chaps kept an eye on him as far as they could, but his activities turned out to be completely innocuous, not to say boring. He'd stay in bed till noon, at least he wouldn't leave his room until that time. Then he'd have lunch and go to the pictures probably, or sit in the hotel lounge reading the newspaper or a magazine. Apart from those visits to the cinema he didn't go much beyond the square. He'd walk round there fairly regularly, and sometimes venture a little way up Swinegate. Waiting for something or somebody, that's what Inspector Duckett said when he told me about it. Of course we'd none of us any idea then who his target was, and even now I can't for the life of me see why anyone should have wanted to have Laura shot. There was just one variation in the routine I've described, and that was that each Sunday he'd get up a little earlier than usual and visit a pub called The Bishop's Move

41

which is quite near where Laura and Jamie lived. But I'll come back to that. This routine went on until the sixth of January, when the sales were in full swing.'

'You're telling me that the streets were crowded when Laura was killed. Are you sure she was the intended victim?'

'That was the first thing that occurred to the police, of course, though they later came to the conclusion that she was. I was interested because of Richard, and I got a good deal of this from Star's Dad. There was no reason from his point of view at that stage why he shouldn't talk to me, though later on naturally enough he closed up like a clam.'

'I can understand that, but tell me as much as you can.'

'All this keeping of observation strained the detective branch's resources to the limit, as I expect you can imagine,' Chris went on, 'and they were driven to co-opting some of the uniformed division constables, putting them into plain clothes, and setting them to work as well. That's how Jim Ryder came to be on duty that day and a pretty boring job he had of it, I should think, not even a visit to the cinema. Porson didn't budge from the hotel until just before five o'clock, but when he did he moved quickly, and Jim lost sight of him when he turned into the ginnel behind the Imperial Café.'

'You'd better not let any of our witnesses say that, it's just the sort of thing the judge would want explaining.'

'Especially as we've got Gilmour again,' Chris agreed. 'Yes, I thought that would please you. We'll make it alley if you prefer. It's just about wide enough to take two people abreast when it leaves the square, and though it widens out a little behind the buildings there's no way for traffic to reach it, which makes it awkward for deliveries and so on. In fact, there've been a number of complaints . . . but that's beside the point.'

'Yes, I don't think even Mr Justice Gilmour would need quite so much detail,' said Maitland thoughtfully. 'Go on, Chris. Jim had just lost sight of his quarry.'

'You'll remember the Imperial — it's a three-storey

building fronting on the square – but I don't suppose you know that the two upper floors are flats, and there's a fire escape running up the back. It was dark, of course, and Jim just didn't see him going up. I don't think you can blame him, it wasn't his sort of job at all, following people about, and I don't think he could have done anything in any case. What seems to have happened is that Porson got in through a landing window on the top floor, from there there's a ladder that lets down and a trap-door leading to the roof.'

'That's rather odd, isn't it? Had he had any opportunity of exploring the ground?'

'The police say he hadn't, but one of them may be covering up his own lack of observation. Or his principal may have cased the joint for him. However that may be, Porson certainly got on to the roof and shot Laura Willard from there.'

'How did he know –?'

'Wait for it, Antony, don't be so impatient. Since Jamie was old enough to be left to his own devices for an hour or two Laura had been in the habit of taking a temporary job during the sales at Bardsey's, which you may or may not remember is the biggest department store in town. She used to work in the lingerie department, but she always left promptly at five, and walked down Swinegate into the square to catch the bus home. She was a creature of habit and he could be quite sure of seeing her there at that precise moment.'

'Three things. If Porson didn't know he was being followed your local police deserve a pat on the back.'

'Yes, I think so too, but he can't have known, can he? I know he'd be wary, but he wouldn't expect anyone to be interested in him so far off his own beat.'

'I suppose not. The next thing is, what if Laura had stopped to do some shopping?'

'He could have waited for her, but I gather there was no question of that. She always did her shopping locally, I mean near her home, and if she had wanted to take advantage of a

43

special rate for anything from Bardsey's I daresay she'd look after that during the lunch hour. Anyway the people who saw her go down had no idea at first what had happened – I suppose they took the crack of the shot for a car back-firing – but when all the statements were sorted out it seemed pretty obvious that there'd been nobody near her on the pavement at the precise moment she was hit. That was one thing, besides the fact that she was the only person around who could have been expected to be there at that precise moment each evening, that convinced the police from the beginning she was the intended victim. There were also the visits to the pub I told you about, and the walks up Swinegate where Bardsey's is situated, which might have been to familiarise himself with her route home.'

'Which brings me to my third point, though I think it's answered itself already. It seems obvious that someone who knew Laura well was Porson's informant, in which case I suppose a photograph might have been provided to help him recognise her.'

'You're going too fast for me again,' said Chris amiably. 'That, as it turned out, was the clincher. They didn't get round to searching his room at the hotel at once, but when they did they found a snapshot of Laura and Jamie – one of those things street photographers take and then try to sell you. It was a very good likeness of them both.'

'Back to Constable Ryder then.'

'Yes, poor chap. He heard the shot too and in the light of his knowledge wasn't in any doubt what it was or where it came from, so he went to the bottom of the fire escape and just waited for Porson to come down. Well, we both know he wasn't the brightest of fellows, Antony, and if he'd just concealed himself –'

'I think it was very brave of him,' said Star.

'Nobody's denying that. Anyway, the long and the short of it was that Porson shot him too, though I daresay he was a little rattled at being challenged because for once he didn't make a clean job of it, and Jim didn't die immediately. He wasn't found straight away, and was very near death when Superintendent Morrison reached him. But he was able to say enough to make it quite certain that Porson was the killer, only by that time, of course, the chap had gone to ground. He's in a bad position because when he shows his face again there's Jim Ryder's dying deposition. A doctor's car was stolen that evening and abandoned in Leeds and the police think he got away in that. Anyway they've found no trace of him yet.'

'Laura was killed instantly?'

'Yes, she was shot through the head. You'll find all the particulars in your brief.'

'It never occurred to anyone that Porson might have had a personal motive?'

'I don't see how it could have been that. There's no record anywhere of Porson ever having been to Arkenshaw before and I don't think he could have been without the London police knowing at least that he was away from his usual haunts, unless it was quite some time ago. More than the seven years that Richard and Laura have been separated anyway. And I told you Laura lived a very quiet life.'

'Did she never go away?'

'Not without Jamie. They'd go to the seaside, usually Scarborough from what Richard told me, for a month in the summer; Richard is quite sure she never went to London.'

'She might not have wanted him to know.'

'He saw too much of Jamie, and even if the boy had been told to hide the fact from his father, Richard's quite sure he'd have known something was wrong. Well, not wrong, but that Jamie was hiding something from him.'

'The police therefore decided that Porson was acting for somebody else,' said Maitland slowly. 'Somebody who knew Laura intimately, it seems. It isn't everyone who has a professional hit-man on his list of acquaintances.'

'No, that's a difficulty, whoever arranged it.'

'What happened next?'

'The police interviewed Richard and I got a description of

their talk from him. At that time of the evening he wouldn't normally have been on stage, but they were starting a new production that week, someone had fallen ill, and there was a special rehearsal lasting from four o'clock until nearly seven at which he was present. He'd be bound to be the first person they thought of, and that must have made them more suspicious than ever, because if it hadn't been for the fact that Porson was known to be in Arkenshaw, and the further fact that Jim Ryder had identified him as the murderer, that would have seemed like an unbreakable alibi. They couldn't help considering the possibility that the murder had been arranged for that particular evening because Richard knew about this extra rehearsal, and had tipped his agent off.'

'Did he tell the police about the present position between himself and Laura?'

'He said that they were separated, which all their neighbours knew anyway, and that they were now contemplating a divorce. He didn't say anything about the difficulties with Lionel Eardley, or even that it was Laura who wanted the divorce so that she could marry again.'

'You weren't present at this interview, I take it?'

'No, I wasn't. I don't think it ever occurred to Richard that he needed my help about that, ready as he was to confide in me about his other difficulties. To my mind that's a sort of argument for his innocence.'

'Not one that I could use in court.'

'No, I realise that. But you do see what I mean?'

Antony smiled at him. 'I see you're quite convinced yourself of your friend's innocence,' he said.

'As I hope you will be when you've seen him. In the meantime I realise we're asking you to take a lot on trust, Star and I.'

That was perhaps a remark that was better ignored, for the moment at least.

'I can quite see he was the first person the police considered, but I suspect they had a look round for some further possibilities,' Maitland remarked.

'Yes, but I don't know anything about that. And this is one of our worst difficulties I think, Antony . . . the fact that Laura was such an unlikely person to have been murdered.'

'That already occurred to me, from something you said. She had no money of her own, for instance? A financial motive is something the most fat-headed jury can understand.'

'Not according to Richard.'

'I was afraid not. And at this stage, I take it, the police were baffled. They could hardly charge Willard on the mere fact that he'd been married to the dead woman, and that he had an alibi for the time of her death. In any case they didn't proceed immediately to an arrest.'

'No, of course not,' said Chris rather impatiently. 'That was Eardley's doing.'

'You mean he went and told them about his engagement to Laura? If you can talk about an engagement before the divorce was through,' he added doubtfully.

'That and quite a lot more. He told them about Mary Norton, and that neither he nor Laura thought it would be suitable for Richard to see so much of his son in future. A bad example, a bad influence, I don't know how he put it but either way he left no doubt that Richard had a motive, and that he and Laura had had one or two rows on the subject. Which was bad enough. Richard's devotion to Jamie must have been known to a good many people, even if his regular visits didn't demonstrate it by themselves. So now the police were aware that he had an almost perfect motive, but unfortunately that wasn't all.'

'Come on, Chris, out with it!'

'It isn't good,' said Chris reluctantly.

'And you're afraid it will make me agree with the police about Willard's guilt. All the same, I have to know. Ask Star, she understands.'

'A picture of Porson had been circulated by this time,' said Chris. 'It had been on the telly, and in the newspapers. What Eardley said was that from the beginning he'd been quite sure the police would see it his way, that no one but Richard could have been guilty, but as time went on he began to think he'd have to take some action himself. Laura had told him that there was a pub not far from home that Richard was in the habit of visiting, usually if he arrived a bit early on the days he was taking Jamie out. It isn't easy to time one's arrival by car to a minute or two, especially when coming from a distance. Laura and Jamie always went to chapel at eleven o'clock, rather a long service and then the walk home, so she didn't like Richard to get to the house before twelve-thirty. So Eardley got to thinking that perhaps after the rows the two of them had had Richard might have gone into this same place for a quick one to settle his nerves or cheer himself up or however you like to put it. At least, that's the only interpretation I can put on his actions, and I don't really know what he was expecting to discover, perhaps that the demon drink had had such an effect that Richard had regaled the assembled company with a series of threats against his wife. Eardley doesn't approve of drink, though if you remember, Antony, being teetotal isn't necessarily one of the Levellers' things, but he felt he had a duty to Laura's memory – I can just hear him saying that – and anyway he went.'

'And this hostelry, I take it, was The Bishop's Move?'

'It was, and he was quite right – they did know Richard there. The landlord remembered him from the days when he lived just around the corner, and even since he left Arkenshaw he's been a regular visitor, always at the same time, around opening time on Sundays. Anyway the long and the short of it was that he was pretty sure he hadn't seen much of Richard during December, and never at any time in the evening, which wasn't really much help to Eardley, and the landlord flatly refused to take any part in finding out anything more. He didn't even mention that the police had been there already, asking questions, though that happened to be the truth. So Eardley went back on the following Sunday at noon, and started talking about the murder, which naturally round there was rather more than a nine day's wonder. Eventually a chap called Hanbury chipped in, saying he knew Richard well by sight and remembered seeing him there the Sunday before Christmas in earnest conversation with a man with a scarred face. At that point Eardley whipped out a photograph that he'd cut from the newspaper, and Hanbury positively identified Porson as being the man he'd seen, and Eardley persuaded him to go round with him straight away to the police station. And the police renewed their inquiries at The Bishop's Move – the landlord was naturally rather more co-operative with them than he'd been with Eardley, thinking of his licence no doubt – and they were able to dig up a second man who had been there that day and who also remembered the conversation.' Chris stopped and spread his hands. 'Circumstantial evidence, of course, but I should say myself they'd a pretty good *prima facie* case, wouldn't you?'

'I should indeed,' said Antony.

'Now, don't go getting any ideas into your head.'

Again Maitland ignored the invitation to comment. 'Does Willard admit this conversation?' he asked.

'He admits that he was in the pub at that time. He says he always talks to people in pubs if he gets half a chance, and he remembers a man with a scar but didn't think anything of it . . . wasn't even certain which day they'd talked together.'

'Yet surely he took some interest in what had happened to his wife?'

'Of course he did.'

'Then he must have looked with special interest at the pictures in the newspapers and on the television.'

'I daresay he did, all the same he says he didn't make the connection.'

'I see. The other thing is that I got an impression from something you said, Chris, that Willard hadn't been here on that particular Sunday.'

'He didn't stay with us, but –'

'But he had an explanation for that too. I think on the

49

whole I'd rather hear that from himself.' He paused for a moment, thinking. 'You see what this means, don't you . . . both of you?' he demanded. 'If the evidence from the pub is reliable –'

'You can make a good deal of Eardley showing the photograph around before the police came into it.'

'Oh yes, no doubt I can. But do you think the evidence is reliable?'

'I'm afraid so.'

'Had neither of the witnesses recognised Porson's photograph before Eardley showed it to them?'

'Hanbury – whose evidence I imagine will be the most convincing – had been abroad and heard nothing of the matter. He takes his holiday in the winter and goes skiing. The other chap is a bit of an odd-ball, doesn't own a television, and hardly ever opens a newspaper.'

'Some people would say, a sensible chap,' said Maitland absently. 'But what I was going to point out – though I'm quite sure you've seen it for yourself already – is that either Richard Willard is guilty, or somebody has deliberately framed him.'

'Yes, I do see that, of course, but it must be the latter.'

'Even though Porson's presence here was only known to the police by accident? Don't worry about it now,' he added hastily, seeing Chris's downcast look. 'The idea could have been for him to get safely away, and then for the principal plotter to identify him to the police in some way. It might even have been done without their knowing the man with the scar was Porson, by some anonymous person claiming to be an eye-witness who didn't want to get mixed up in anything nasty. But no, I don't think that's likely. Porson must have been a party to the plot from the beginning. For all we know it may have suited his plans very well to go abroad and start a new career.'

'You don't believe a word of that, do you?'

'Don't rush me, Chris. There's another thing I need to know. You said the police had been keeping Porson under observation. Was the chap who was tailing him that Sunday actually in the pub or not?'

'Apparently not. Each time he was followed there his shadow thought it best to stay outside.'

'Tell me about Lionel Eardley.'

'There isn't much to tell. He's the office manager at Comstock's Mill, rather a good-looking chap though I thought he had rather a mean expression. A local man, no brothers or sisters and his parents are dead. According to Richard he'd got Laura exactly where he wanted her. Quite ready to become a Leveller herself, and to follow his lead in everything.'

'For all the good looks you spoke of he doesn't sound exactly the type –' Maitland began doubtfully.

'I expect she was lonely,' said Star.

Chris brushed the explanation aside. 'Yes, I daresay she was, but it was her own doing, wasn't it? I agree with Antony, she ought to have had the sense to see through the chap. But this business of Richard being framed –'

'I don't think we can go into that tonight,' Maitland told him. 'We'll talk again after I've seen Willard. Can you tell me about Laura's family, Chris?'

'Not really, because I only got to know Richard, as I told you, when they were about to separate.'

'You disappoint me.' Maitland smiled again. 'I've always thought,' he confided to Star, 'that Chris knew everything there was to know about Arkenshaw and its inhabitants. Do you think Grandma could help me?'

'I expect she could,' said Star doubtfully.

'Do you mean that she and your father are too cross about what happened to Constable Ryder to want to help?'

'Dad is. He's quite sure Richard's guilty, and can't understand Chris being willing to take the case. But I didn't really mean that about Grandma, though of course she's upset about Jim's death. I really meant she doesn't like talking about other people, particularly if there's anything unkind to say.'

51

'Yes, I know that, all the same I'd like to see her. I would do anyway, you know, even if I wasn't curious about Laura's family, so there can be no harm whatever in arranging it, Chris, and if the talk happens to veer in a certain direction —'

'Yes, I know you, but I know Grandma too,' said Chris. 'What happens when an irresistible force meets an immovable object? But you must certainly come and see Grandma tomorrow afternoon, she'd be dreadfully hurt if you didn't.'

'And what about Inspector Duckett?'

Chris grinned. 'He won't actually throw you out of the house,' he said, 'but naturally he'd consider it dreadfully improper to have any conversation with you at the moment, even though he isn't directly engaged in the prosecution, and even if you stuck to the most harmless subjects.'

'All right then, we'll leave it there. What time in the morning, Chris? I take it that you've arranged for us to see Willard.'

'I'll call for you at the hotel at nine-thirty.'

'Good.' Maitland was on his feet now. 'There's just one thing that I should like to know for my own peace of mind,' he added. 'What's happened to Jamie since his mother died?'

'The local bobby knew there were just the two of them, so the police went first to a neighbour, a motherly sort of soul, and she took him in overnight. Richard rushed over, of course, as soon as he heard, but the police pounced on him before he'd even had the chance to speak to Jamie, and by the time that interview was finished Laura's sister Amanda had arrived and installed herself in the house. I haven't met her, but Richard told me he could quite see that it was the best arrangement for the moment, less upsetting for Jamie than leaving what had always been his home. He said Amanda was quite willing to stay for six months or so, until it seemed reasonable for him to marry Mary and make some permanent arrangement about a home for the boy. As it turned out, of course, it was the best thing that could have happened.'

'Yes, I can see that. Well, I'll see you in the morning then, Chris –'

'And you'll come here to dinner, of course,' said Star. 'After all' – for the moment her smile had all its normal radiance – 'you'll probably need reviving after a session with Grandma.'

Saturday, 1st February

I

Of all the duties connected with his profession, visiting a client in prison was perhaps for Maitland the worst of all. Nor is there anything about the majority of Her Majesty's prisons to elevate either the mind or the spirit, and Wentworth Gaol, on the outskirts of Arkenshaw, was perhaps even less attractive than most. By the time they'd reached the interview room Antony's spirits had reached their lowest ebb, and somehow the memory of the last occasion Chris had brought him here, quite a number of years ago, was suddenly vivid in his mind. This was even the same room. He strolled across to the window, and looked out across Cargate, which is a very long road leading directly out of town. Certainly the view looked the same, though he couldn't possibly remember whether the row of shops opposite had the same occupants. The trams had gone now, though no one had troubled to remove the tracks, and the double decker buses no longer looked unfamiliar. Only, when he had left the hotel that morning and seen the square for the first time that trip in daylight, he had been surprised to see that the cleaning of the more venerable of the soot-encrusted buildings had begun. 'No respect for tradition,' he had grumbled, getting into the car, though secretly he admitted it was an improvement.

There was a fair amount of traffic about, considering it was Saturday morning – *prisons are built with stones of Law* . . . what on earth had put that into his head just at the moment? What he must do now was to keep his mind very firmly fixed on the facts of the case, without allowing the intrusion of the sympathy, which was all too likely to colour his thoughts, particularly in these surroundings. And if he came to the conclusion that Richard Willard was guilty, which would seem on the face of it the most likely thing? *I'll be judge, I'll be jury* . . . that wasn't within his function either. Chris and Star were suffering enough because of their faith in their friend, without having his own scepticism added to their burden.

He didn't turn away from the window until Richard Willard had come into the room and the door had been locked again behind him. Richard had said something in reply to Chris's greeting, and by now Chris was busy with the introductions. But neither of his companions paid much heed, they were taking stock of each other. Maitland saw a man as tall as himself, not conventionally good-looking but certainly sufficiently so to be cast as leading man in most plays, rather than being condemned perpetually to character parts. His hair was a little longer than that of either of his companions, which might have been his own taste, or called for by whatever part he was playing at the time of his arrest. It was straight, and of a colour that Antony mentally described to himself as dark mouse though it was quite obvious that Willard had been recently running his fingers through it. His eyes were blue and he had a candid look which would make a good impression on the jury if it weren't followed by the inevitable thought: After all, the man's an actor. But Maitland also saw, as though he'd been looking at a reflection of what his own feelings might have been under similar circumstances, that his confinement was already beginning to tell on him.

Willard on the other hand saw in his counsel in those first moments the last thing that he had expected – something approaching nervousness. This was a sensitive man, he realised immediately, perhaps too sensitive for his own good. And he thought, only able to manage a brief flicker of interest in something beyond his immediate predicament, that if he had been playing the barrister in a comparable scene on the

55

stage his attitude would have been very, very different. Self-confident, in fact. But then Maitland was coming forward, and his tone was matter-of-fact, his manner casual, and the momentary impression was forgotten.

Chris said, with uncharacteristic uncertainty, 'I've been telling Mr Maitland a good deal about the facts of the case, but I think there are still a few questions he'd like you to answer yourself.' His attitude could only have been due to his wondering what kind of an impression Richard was going to make on his counsel, and Antony responded by saying as reassuringly as he could and with rather more formality than he generally used on these occasions (the formalities being in his opinion the business of his instructing solicitor),

'I'm sorry we have to meet under such unfortunate circumstances, Mr Willard. From what Chris tells me I'm surprised my wife and I haven't run into you sometimes on our visits to Arkenshaw.'

'You always come in the summer,' Chris reminded him. 'And Richard's visits aren't always so regular then, because he may be working further away.'

'Yes, of course.' About as meaningless a comment as he could have devised if he had been deliberately attempting to be as trite as he could, but the best he could manage at the moment. 'Why don't we all sit down,' he suggested. For himself he would have preferred to remain standing and free to roam about the room at will, but there was the question first of trying to get their client to relax a little.

'I'm afraid,' said Willard with an attempt at a lighter tone, 'that I can't exactly offer you home comforts.' He looked ruefully for a moment at the hard wooden chairs, and then pulled one out and seated himself at the end of the table. Maitland took the chair opposite him, with Chris sitting between as though to act as referee. 'I expect Chris told you that the police have got it all wrong.'

'Yes, he told me that, and so did Star, very vehemently,' said Antony smiling. That was the first good mark for his client, the attempt – slight though it was – at humour.

56

'Then I don't really see what else there is for me to tell you.'

'Come now, Mr Willard, you must see I need something to take into court besides a straight denial. I gather the police have a witness who will testify that you quarrelled with your wife. Do you admit that?'

'That chap Eardley,' said Richard in a tone of loathing. 'About the first occasion he can only say what Laura told him; that's hearsay evidence, isn't it?'

'Yes, but I'm afraid as your wife is now deceased it would be admissable,' Maitland explained. 'The question is, what will you have to tell the court yourself on that issue?'

'I can't deny it.'

'Tell me, then,' Maitland invited.

'Each time it was on a Sunday when I came over from Rothershaw to see Jamie. Laura had never made any difficulty about my visits, but because she took him to chapel in the morning she didn't like me to arrive until about half-past twelve. It was the first of December that brought the change in the usual order of things. Laura and I had never quarrelled, but there wasn't much to say to each other after all those years apart, unless it concerned Jamie, so usually I just went as far as the door and collected him and when I took him home I'd wait at the gate until he got into the house. But that day Laura came to the door herself and told Jamie, who was hovering in the hall, to wait in the kitchen because she wanted to talk to me. I thought it must be something about his schooling, perhaps he'd made up his mind what he wanted to do when he grew up and needed to take some special courses, something like that. After all, he's twelve now. So we went into the sitting room, and as soon as she'd shut the door she said quite abruptly that she wanted a divorce.'

'Did that surprise you?'

'I suppose the answer to that is, yes and no. I mean, I wasn't expecting it, but when I thought it over afterwards it seemed to me that there was no reason for me to have been

57

taken aback. My first reaction was to be pleased about it, because I took it for granted it meant she wanted to marry again but in any event it would clear the way for me to marry Mary – did Chris tell you about Mary? – and I never thought of it making any difference to the arrangements about seeing Jamie as often as I could.'

'You asked her why she wanted the divorce, I suppose?'

'Yes, naturally, and she told me she'd met someone she wanted to marry, a man called Lionel Eardley, and she intended to bring a suit against me citing Mary as co-respondent.'

'Wait a bit! Had you confided in Laura about your relationship with Miss Norton?'

'No, I hadn't, it's hardly the sort of thing one talks about with one's wife even after so many years' separation. So the first thing I asked her was how did she know, and she said that Lionel had told her. He'd made it his business to find out apparently, because he knew all people in the theatrical profession led irregular lives, and I'm afraid I said rather sarcastically, "Quite the little detective, isn't he?" At which she flared up and said that it was just as well to know the true state of affairs, and that things would be very different in future. That was when everything began to go wrong.'

'Did she go on to tell you what she meant by that?'

'Yes. She said, about Jamie. But before that she told me that Lionel was a Leveller. I'd never heard of them, but Chris tells me they're a sort of religious sect, with very strict ideas, and that they have a chapel here in Arkenshaw. Laura told me she was very impressed by what Lionel had told her about them, she and Jamie had been there that morning and would be going in future, and of course there was no question of my going on seeing Jamie as long as I was living in sin. She actually said that. So I pointed out that if these Levellers believed in divorce, as it seemed they did, I shouldn't be living in sin anyway once the decree was made absolute because I should marry Mary, but Laura said she'd make a fight for it when the hearing came on, there was no question

58

of my getting custody because any judge could see that it would be difficult for me to make a proper home for Jamie, and she was quite sure my visiting rights would be very much less generous than she'd allowed in the past, and she and Lionel would see that they were strictly adhered to. By that time I'd lost my temper and I'm afraid we just shouted whatever insults we could think of at each other for the next few minutes.'

'You're very devoted to your son, aren't you, Mr Willard?'

'Is there anything wrong with that?'

'On the contrary. But Chris will explain to you – I expect he has already – that one can't start to prepare a defence unless one knows the very worst that can be said by the prosecution. And unless I'm very much mistaken they'll be using your affection for Jamie to explain your motive.'

'Yes, I see that. I was livid, of course, it wasn't only about not seeing Jamie so often, though that was at the top of the list, I suppose. Laura said some pretty rotten things about Mary, I think she was quoting Eardley but that didn't make it any better. And I didn't want Jamie to be brought up in one of these crackpot religions, particularly as Laura seemed to be completely under Eardley's thumb, and the pair of them were likely to enforce an over-strict code of conduct on him. In fact, she said as much. And she said that even if the court was misguided enough to allow me to see him sometimes, she'd make very sure he wasn't corrupted by the kind of life I led. I could hardly believe my ears as a matter of fact, because it wasn't at all like Laura. It was almost as if this chap had bewitched her.'

'I think perhaps we'd better leave witchcraft out of it, Mr Willard. It doesn't sound the sort of argument the court would give any credence to.'

'No, it was just a manner of speaking. I was beginning to be afraid that they'd try to mould Jamie's future into some form that he wouldn't like at all, so I pointed out that as long as I was paying for his education I expected to have some say in it. But Laura said that she wouldn't need my help any longer, and as for Jamie if the court made an order – as she was sure they would – for his maintenance, she'd be free to spend it as she liked. She must have got all that from Eardley, she'd never have thought it out for herself.'

'Has Jamie any idea yet of what line he wants to follow? In your footsteps perhaps?'

'I know he's thought about that, but I've always had the idea that he might become a writer.'

'A journalist?'

'No, I meant a novelist of some sort. He has a very vivid imagination, and gift for words. But of course, I wouldn't dream of making any such suggestion to him, I just wanted to make sure he got the best arts education he could – because obviously he's not cut out for any of the sciences – and then leave it up to him to make up his own mind.'

'I'm told it's not a very easy profession to make your way in, particularly at first.'

'I realise that, but I'd be quite willing to back him as long as he needed it. Mary intends to go on working, so I don't think we shall be hard up. Should have been, I should say.'

'How did your visit end?'

'I went out into the hall and slammed the door, and Jamie was standing in the kitchen doorway; he'd been listening to the noise we made, I suppose. So I just said, "Come along," and before Laura had time to stop him we were out of the front door and down the street. We usually go – went – to the Midland Hotel for lunch, because there are not too many places open on a Sunday, and of course Jamie's not old enough for me to take him for a pub lunch. So that's what we did that day as well and we didn't talk at all in the car on the way there, except that Jamie asked me in a rather small voice whether his mother and I were very angry with each other, and I'm afraid I just said, "Yes!" and left it at that. By the time we got to our usual table I'd calmed down a bit and I asked him whether he knew Laura wanted to marry again. He said he did, so I asked him right out what he thought of having this man Eardley as a stepfather.'

60

'And what did he have to say to that?'

'He said, "I hate him!" I shan't have to tell the court that, shall I?'

'That, I'm afraid, will depend on Counsel for the Prosecution. If he demands a full account of your conversation with Jamie –'

'Yes, I see that. I'm not a particularly religious man, Mr Maitland, but I'm not prepared to lie on oath. And not just because perjury is against the law.'

'Thank you for telling me that.'

'Then, from what you said just now, I take it you want to know the whole thing too.'

'I'm afraid I do.'

'Well, Jamie thought Eardley was . . . smarmy I think was the word he used. And he said Laura had changed completely, not the loving person she'd always been but seeming to be terrified of spoiling him. He didn't use those words, of course, I'm just giving you the gist of what he said. The morning was the first time they'd been to the Levellers' service – he hated that too. Not that I think he ever cared for chapel anyway. If Jamie turns out to be religious I think he'll want something with a bit more mysticism about it. So I asked him if Laura or Eardley had ever been unkind to him, and he said, "not exactly," but they'd told him he'd be seeing less of me in the future, and Eardley had said what a wicked place the stage was, and that Jamie had bad blood in his veins – what a thing to say to a child – but that they'd make very sure that he trod the – the path of righteousness from now on. Now I *am* quoting, the phrase seemed to have stuck in Jamie's mind.'

'And no wonder.'

'Eardley'd said too that their plans for him – his and Laura's – involved putting aside any idea of higher education, in fact any idea of staying at school after the minimum leaving age. He would have to take some wretched job as a clerk. Not that I've anything against working in an office, I suppose you could say Eardley has done pretty well

61

for himself, but it would be against Jamie's temperament, he'd be miserable doing anything that involved that sort of routine.'

'Had all this arisen since the last time you saw him? When was that by the way?'

'Only the week before. No, Eardley had been visiting the house for some months, Jamie hadn't liked him but he'd no idea where the visits were going to lead so he didn't think them important enough to mention to me. But then the previous Tuesday Laura had told him that she and Lionel had decided to marry as soon as her divorce from me went through, and after that Eardley had taken several opportunities to have what he called "little talks" with Jamie. By this time I'd got mad all over again, though I tried to hide it as well as I could, and I told him things might not turn out to be as bad as he thought, and anyway I'd make very sure we went on seeing each other. I wasn't at all sure about that, I can tell you, but I didn't want to turn him against his mother.'

'And after that?'

'We went for a drive, and I took him home at the usual time, and then went to Chris's.'

'But you didn't say anything about this quarrel?'

'No, because I thought . . . well, Eardley sounded such an unattractive chap I couldn't believe Laura's feelings for him would last. I hoped they might quarrel, and everything would get back to normal. But the next week when I drove over I found Jamie waiting for me outside The Bishop's Move. It was bitterly cold and he looked frozen stiff, but he just said he thought it would be a better idea to meet me there rather than have me come to the house. Only of course I questioned him about it, and I found he'd been wandering around since just after breakfast, when he slipped away from home rather than go to that confounded chapel again. And he said Laura had been furious with him when he got back the previous week, and told him he mustn't see me again; but he wanted to explain to me that if they stopped him it wasn't because *he* wanted to give up our outings; and besides there was a question he wanted to ask me. And when I said, "What was that?" he asked me what a whore was.' He paused there looking from one of his companions to the other. 'They'd told him about Mary,' he said, 'and that's the word Eardley had used. I . . . well, to be honest with you, I think at that moment I could have strangled Laura if she'd been anywhere near, and this wretched man she'd taken up with as well, but I did my best to explain the position to Jamie, and I think I must have done fairly well because when I'd finished he said, why couldn't he come and live with us? So then there was a lot more explaining to do – I told him I'd talk to Chris about the situation but I couldn't bring myself to hold out any false hopes. On the whole it wasn't a very happy day, but I insisted on taking him right home so that I could try to persuade Laura that the whole thing had been my idea . . . his sneaking away like that, I mean. Only Eardley was with her and it just led to another no-holds-barred row. I don't think it helped the situation at all. And of course once I saw the two of them together and listened to Eardley positively spitting venom, and saw Laura hanging on his words I knew just how serious the situation was. And if you're going to ask me why I didn't tell Chris that evening, it was because I just couldn't bring myself to do so. There we were, Chris and Star and young Tony, and they were so contented. I knew I'd have to talk to him sooner or later, and I suppose it was cowardly to put it off again, but that's what I did.'

'Until the next week?'

'Yes. I'd told Jamie the best thing for us to do was to lie low until after the divorce hearing – there wasn't any point in getting him into trouble. That Sunday I just went straight to Chris and told him the whole thing. Of course it was still up in the air, the divorce papers weren't served until the following week and no one could foretell how the court would see things, but he didn't really hold out very much hope that it would go the way I wanted.'

'So we come to Sunday the twenty-second. Was that the date? The Sunday before Christmas anyway.'

'Yes. I'd told Chris I wasn't coming, but at the last moment I thought I'd have one more try at talking some sense into Laura. So I came over at the usual time, but then I thought I'd better wait till they'd finished their lunch and so I went to The Bishop's Move and stayed there a bit longer than usual.'

'And that's when you talked to the man Porson, who later shot your wife.'

'I talked to all sorts of people, but there was a man with a scar on his face who told me he'd heard I was an actor, and asked if I could give him some advice on behalf of his son who was thinking of going on the stage. Well, you can imagine that was the last thing I wanted to do, but it seemed as good a way of passing the time as any so we went to a table by the window and I did my best to explain to him the very certain difficulties and only problematical rewards of the profession. I suppose we had quite a long talk, though my mind wasn't exactly on it.'

'The man with the scar has been identified as Porson. In any case there wouldn't be much doubt about it as he was followed to the pub by the police. I'm wondering why you didn't recognise him when the man-hunt got under way and his picture was plastered all over the newspapers and was shown on television.'

Willard looked at him for a long moment, but when finally he spoke it seemed spontaneously enough. 'Because I . . . after all, I had been married to Laura, and even if we'd been on bad terms recently I wasn't quite unmoved by her death. I deliberately avoided any reference to it in the media. Does that seem so very strange?' he added challengingly.

'Even though you must have known that in the circumstances you'd be bound to be the principal suspect?'

'Even so. *I* knew I'd had nothing to do with what had happened.'

'Very well then, we'll leave it there. You were going to tell me what happened after you left The Bishop's Move.'

'I waited until two o'clock before going round to the house, but my idea of talking quietly to Laura was a washout, because Eardley was there. So that was just another row, and on thinking it over – you've a lot of time to think in here – I suppose that was when he got the idea of going round to the pub and making inquiries, because I remember he said at one point something about my having the nerve to expect to see my son when I came to the house reeking of drink. If he really thought I'd had a little too much – which I hadn't – he may have hoped I'd been making threats against Laura, because he couldn't possibly have expected to get the evidence he did . . . that I'd been talking to her actual murderer.'

'Not unless he'd arranged that encounter himself,' said Chris, interrupting for the first time.

'Do you think that might have been it? No, what earthly reason would he have had for killing her, or rather for wanting her dead, when they'd only just arranged to be married?'

'From what you tell us about him,' said Antony slowly, 'if he'd found some real or imagined cause for complaint against her conduct he might well have reacted violently. It's certainly something we'll have to look into.'

'But I tell you, he had Laura completely where he wanted her.'

'Well, at the very least it's a question he'll have to answer in court,' said Antony. 'What took him to the pub, and what evidence he expected to find there. Though I wouldn't want to raise any hopes about the kind of answer I'll get when I ask him. But there's one thing you haven't told me, Mr Willard. Had you ever seen Edwin Porson before?'

'Not that I remember.'

'Yet he seems to have had a pretty good idea that you'd be at The Bishop's Move. If his being there and talking to you was a deliberate attempt to frame you, that is.'

'You think that I –' Willard broke off and looked at him

helplessly. 'I should have realised when you asked me about my not having recognised his picture. Of course, there's no reason why you should believe me any more than anyone else will, but I'd like to ask you one thing. How do you suppose I knew where to get hold of a professional killer?'

'I'm afraid that difficulty applies to whoever instigated the murder.'

'You don't believe me,' said Richard flatly.

'I didn't say so.'

'Not in so many words.' He looked at Chris. 'Is there any point in going on with this?' he asked.

Maitland answered before Conway could speak. 'There's every reason,' he said sharply. 'Did you see Jamie that day?'

Again Willard hesitated before he replied. 'No,' he said at last.

'And you didn't go to see Chris and Star when you left Laura and Eardley together.'

'Not that day. I was terribly angry, and in some odd way ashamed. Not because I'd tried to make Laura see reason but because I'd failed so completely. As for seeing Jamie' – it had been touch and go, but he seemed to have decided that a policy of frankness with his counsel would be best – 'I'd told him not to expect me, so I just went straight back to Rothershaw.'

'Then we must come to the next point. Who else besides yourself might have had a motive for wanting Laura dead? Leaving aside your friend Mr Eardley for a moment.'

Richard might have decided on frankness but still he took his time about answering. He seemed to be considering what motive lay behind the question. 'To tell you the truth I'd rather not leave him on one side,' he said at last, 'though I can quite see . . . oh, well! The trouble is I find it utterly impossible to think of anyone who'd want to be rid of her. Until she came under his influence she was such a nice person. I'd stopped loving her, but I wasn't blind to her good qualities.'

'Chris tells me you don't think Porson could have known

her, could have had any personal motive for what he did.'

'Again I wish I could say that wasn't so, but unless they met here, which Chris tells me the police say is very unlikely, I don't see how they could have known one another. Jamie and I didn't talk about Laura's day-to-day doings, but he'd certainly have told me if she'd been away. Besides, I don't think Porson can be the kind of man ... though after meeting Eardley I'm bound to admit Laura's judgement of the opposite sex wasn't all it should have been. And considering she once thought enough of me to marry me, you can make what you like out of that,' he added, with a note of defiance in his voice.

'People change,' said Maitland vaguely. 'You don't know anything about Laura's friends then?'

'No, I don't.'

'Surely some people you knew when you were together –'

'I don't think so. One of the things she told me when we were quarrelling was that all the couples we'd known had dropped her after I left her. Which I thought was a bit thick, considering the whole thing was her idea.'

Again Chris intervened. 'Perhaps the woman next door, Mrs Daphne Lawson, might be able to help us there, Antony.'

'Yes, perhaps she might. Now, Mr Willard, when did you first hear of your wife's death?'

'When I came off stage that Monday evening.'

'Yet I gather she was killed shortly after five o'clock. Had she no identification on her?'

'That wasn't the trouble. There was a letter from her sister in her handbag, and luckily the police had the sense to talk to the chaps who cover that area so they were told that Jamie would be alone. They went to this Mrs Lawson Chris spoke of, and she broke what had happened to him and gave him his supper and a bed for the night. But she told them Laura never spoke of me, although she knew there was a husband living somewhere who was an actor and who visited Jamie regularly. *He* could have told them, of course, but Mrs

67

Lawson seems to be a kind soul and wouldn't let them near him that evening, so it wasn't until Amanda arrived that they knew where I was and were able to telephone the Rothershaw police to tell me what had happened.'

'Amanda is your wife's sister, I believe?'

'That's right, Amanda Hargreaves.'

'Does she live locally? You see I'm wondering how she got out to the spot so quickly.'

'No, she works in Northdean, but she was coming here anyway to spend a few days' holiday with Laura. She arrived about half past nine, and decided with Mrs Lawson that they wouldn't disturb Jamie that night as he was already asleep. But of course Amanda was able to tell the police where I was and they sent someone round to the theatre to inform me.'

'And – ?'

'Well, of course, I got the car and came straight over. Amanda was waiting up for me. I haven't seen her for years but she was quite willing to stay for a while and look after Jamie, and we both agreed that would be best for him until I could make some proper arrangements. And then . . . well, obviously, I'm not in a position to do that, but Chris assures me Amanda's willing to stay on until we see how things turn out.'

'Is she Laura's only relation?'

'No, there's a brother, though I haven't seen him for years either. Henry Hargreaves. He lives in Cartwright Avenue, the other side of town from Laura.'

'Is he married?'

'Yes, his wife's name is Maria.'

'Wouldn't it have been more natural for them to take over the care of Jamie?'

'I suppose it would, but as it happened they were away at the time. They'd spent the New Year with her people in Stavethorpe, and meant to stay on until the following weekend. Of course they returned as soon as they heard what had happened, and offered to take Jamie in. But Amanda can be quite stubborn for such a gentle person. I don't want to get into a fight with anybody but I have to agree with her that Jamie will be best in his own home for the moment. So that's how it's left.'

'I see.' Maitland got to his feet, pushing the chair back so abruptly that it almost toppled over. 'I don't think there's much more we can do for the moment, Mr Willard, though Chris will be seeing you again, of course. Do you realise how quickly this matter may come to trial?'

'Yes, Chris explained it to me.'

'How do you feel about that?'

'I don't want to prolong the agony, but –'

'*He either fears his fate too much,*' said Maitland with a questioning note in his voice.

'Yes, that's it exactly. I ought to be thinking it's better to know the worst, but when that may mean that I know I'm going to be shut up for years . . . to cap your quotation, there's one about conscience making cowards of us all, isn't there? Will you take my word for it that it isn't conscience in my case? Though I'll admit to the cowardice.'

Antony smiled at him, but the smile did not reach his eyes. 'The prospect is enough to daunt anybody,' he said noncommittally. But now he was urgent to be gone and Chris, sensing his mood, did not linger over their farewells. 'Damn you, Chris,' said Maitland as the final gate clanged to behind them. He took a deep breath as though of relief. Cargate was a busy and not very attractive street, but at least it represented freedom. 'What the hell did you want to get me mixed up in this for?'

'You don't believe what Richard told you,' said Chris despondently. 'I was afraid you mightn't.'

'That wouldn't matter,' Antony told him, 'if I were quite certain of either his guilt or innocence. Once or twice I thought . . . but how can I be sure of anything? The evidence from the pub . . . how do you get round that?'

'Then I take it,' said Chris, stopping beside the car but making no move to get in, 'that you'll be going back to town until I let you know the exact date we'll be in court. And meanwhile studying your brief . . . I hope,' he added, not very optimistically.

'You've been talking to Geoffrey Horton,' said Antony unmoved. 'I always study my brief,' he added, not altogether convincingly, 'but I don't see why that should preclude me from forming my own opinion about the people concerned. In any case . . . give me time to think it over, Chris. I can't do anything until tomorrow anyway. I want to see Grandma, and Star's invited me to dinner . . . remember?'

'So she did. I'll take you back to the hotel,' Chris offered, 'then I have to have lunch at the Club with a client who's far too busy to see me during working hours. Can you amuse yourself until about three o'clock? I'll call for you then to take you up to Old Peel House.'

'I think I might manage that,' said Maitland gravely. 'And meanwhile I'll give some serious thought to the question of whether I go or stay tomorrow.'

II

Going into the hotel lobby Maitland had no other thought in his mind than that a drink before lunch would be pleasant, and might possibly get the bad taste of prison visiting out of his mouth. As he went towards the lounge he was hailed by the clerk at the reception desk, and changed course to see what he had to say. 'There's a boy been asking for you, Mr Maitland. I told him I couldn't say when you'd be in, but he said that didn't matter he'd wait just the same. As a matter of fact' – he lowered his voice – 'I know who it is, the Willard boy.' He paused, watching Maitland's expression. 'You don't want to see him,' he said. 'I'll get rid of him for you if you like.'

'No. No, of course I'll see him. Where is he?'

'Over there.' He gestured towards the other side of the lobby. 'Are you sure, Mr Maitland –?' But Antony had already turned away.

There were several sofas against the wall but only one was occupied, or rather had been occupied because Jamie Willard was already on his feet. Obviously he had heard the clerk speaking and he still looked hesitant and did not attempt to come forward. He was a tall boy for his age and painfully thin, his wrists protruding a little from the sleeves of his jacket and his trousers a fraction too short. But what shook Maitland to the depths of his being was the boy's likeness to his father, which, even allowing for the difference in their ages, was quite startling. Only when he spoke, the uncanny resemblance was shattered. 'Are you Mr Maitland?' he asked.

'Yes, I am, and I think you must be Jamie Willard. You're very like your father, you know.'

'Am I? I couldn't hear what he was saying except when he called to you' – a jerk of his head indicated the desk clerk – 'but I thought perhaps he'd told you who I am.'

'He did, but I'd have known anyway as soon as I got a good look at you. I saw your father this morning, you know. He's really very well.' (And may God forgive me for a liar.)

'Did he send me a message?'

'He didn't know I was going to see you.'

'No, of course not, but perhaps you can tell me, Mr Maitland . . . does he blame me for what's happened?'

'I don't understand, Jamie. How could he blame you?'

'Because . . . oh, because I said so much to him about how dreadful it would be to have to live with Mr Eardley.'

This was obviously a good deal more complicated than he had thought. 'I can assure you, Jamie, there's nothing like that in your father's mind. But you want to talk to me?' Jamie nodded violently. 'Does your aunt know you're here?'

'No, I just came. I was afraid she'd think it was silly of me but Tony's always told me –'

'Tony Conway?'

'Yes. He's very young, of course, but a good kid, and he's

71

talked quite a lot about you.'

'He's called after me, did you know that?'

'He rather boasts about it,' said Jamie, in the indulgent tone of a grown man speaking of a child, so that Maitland smiled suddenly and then was as instantly serious again. 'Do you mind my coming?' Jamie added, suddenly anxious.

'Not a bit, I think it's a very good idea for us to have a talk. Supposing we have lunch, your father told me he often brought you here at weekends. But I really think we ought to ring your aunt first in case she's worried.'

'Will you do that, Mr Maitland? Not that I think she'll be cross with me, she's not that sort of person, but if *you* told her it was an – inspiration on my part, then perhaps she wouldn't think it was quite so daft of me to have come here.'

'I'll tell her I think that the word inspiration is inadequate,' Antony promised solemnly, and made off towards the row of telephones at the back of the lobby. The call was answered on the first ring, so that he wondered whether Amanda Hargreaves had actually been sitting beside the machine waiting for news. He introduced himself, told her that Jamie was with him and that he was glad of the opportunity to talk to the boy.

'Was it your idea or his?' Her voice sounded amused, certainly not angry.

'His idea, but I think it's a good one because it has saved me a lot of bother.'

'You wanted to talk to him?' She sounded surprised.

'Yes, of course.' To tell the truth it had never occurred to him to do so, and he wasn't looking forward to the conversation, but there was no point in letting Jamie down by admitting that. 'I thought we could have lunch together. Is that all right with you?'

'Quite all right, if you're sure that's what you want.'

'I'll bring him home afterwards, and then perhaps we can have a short talk, you and I.'

'You're really taking this thing seriously, then?'

'I always take my work seriously.' In spite of himself the

72

words came out a little stiffly.

'Of course you do! I didn't mean to offend you,' she told him, quickly contrite. 'It's just . . . well, it isn't the way most barristers work.'

'I'm the despair of all my friends,' said Antony, and let the amusement show in his voice by way of making amends. 'But seriously, Miss Hargreaves –'

'Yes, of course, I want to help if only for Jamie's sake.'

'Then we'll get an early lunch, right away in fact, and be with you, I hope at about one-thirty.'

'That's fine. Tell Jamie I've forgiven him for doing a disappearing trick. To tell you the truth I wasn't too worried, Laura used to say he was quite good at doing that when he felt like it.'

'I'll tell him.'

He was smiling as he rejoined the boy. 'All is forgiven,' he told him.

'That's good.'

'And Miss Hargreaves quite sees the importance of our talking together,' Antony assured him. 'Come along now, it's early enough for us to be able to choose a table where we can talk in peace.'

If the waiter was surprised to see them together he gave no sign, and he greeted Jamie like an old friend without any undercurrent in his tone that might have reminded him of the present situation. Not, Antony thought rather sadly, that the boy needed any reminding. He had perhaps gained a little reassurance from their brief conversation, but his composure was obviously still hardly held.

When Jamie had been supplied with ginger ale and Maitland with whisky and water, Antony waited a moment until it was obvious that the boy wasn't going to speak without prompting and then asked, 'Well now, Jamie, what did you want to see me about?'

'About my father, of course.'

'Yes, I think I guessed that. But what exactly –?'

Jamie took a sip of his ginger ale as though he felt it had

some strengthening quality, but he wasn't looking at his companion when he replied with apparent irrelevance, 'Tony says you've been here three times before on a case, though it was when he was too young to remember. And each time you were able to help the people you were defending. One of them was his grandfather, Inspector Duckett, but that was before Mr and Mrs Conway were even married.'

'I hope I shall be able to help your father, Jamie.'

'Yes, but I was afraid when you knew how he and my mother had quarrelled you'd just give up without trying very hard.'

'I think I'd better explain something to you, Jamie. When a lawyer takes a criminal case it isn't up to him to be judge and jury, his job is to hear his client's story, and if the client is pleading Not Guilty to put up the best case he can for him in court.'

'But sometimes . . . I mean *you* don't always just leave it there, do you? So I wanted to know whether you were going straight back to London now that you'd seen Dad and Mr Conway, or whether you're going to stay.'

'When did you last see your father, Jamie?' The picture that haunts every English childhood came vividly to his mind as he spoke, but he repressed it sternly and concentrated on his companion's reply.

'At the beginning of December. Mother told me I mustn't see him any more, but I sneaked out of the house and waited for him. And I told him –' He broke off there, his eyes fixed doubtfully on Maitland's face.

'You'd better tell me, Jamie,' Antony prompted him, 'now that you've gone so far.'

'I thought if you understood it was all my fault it might make you more . . . more sympathetic.'

The answer to that ought to have been that sympathy has no place in the relationship between counsel and client, as his uncle had so often reminded him. But somehow the thing that was foremost in Maitland's mind was the echo of his own thought earlier that day: it isn't up to me to be judge and jury. 'I think I'd better tell you, Jamie, before we go any further, that I'm staying in Arkenshaw at least for a day or two. Though there aren't many people I can usefully see . . . I'm not allowed to talk to the prosecution witnesses until we get into court, did you know that?'

'That means' – the boy's face was suddenly radiant – 'it means *you* don't think that Dad had Mother killed.'

No need to give a direct answer to that. 'Is that what you've been thinking?' Antony asked gently.

'No, I –' He started positively enough, but the lie stuck in his throat. 'I didn't want to believe it, Mr Maitland, but they were so angry with each other. And when I saw him that day, the day I told you about, he didn't say much but I knew he was furious, and I told him I couldn't bear the thought of Mr Eardley marrying Mother, so of course I wondered.'

'Before we go any further you'd better think this out,' Antony told him. 'I think you'll find those doubts of yours arise from the feeling you mentioned to me, that you were somehow to blame. And then I think you must consider what you know of your father. Could he have done such a thing in quite so cold-blooded a way? I don't want to force you to think about what happened, but it was carefully planned, not the result of a moment's anger.'

Jamie looked at him for a long, long time and then brushed his hand across his eyes. 'You're right, of course,' he said. 'I haven't been thinking straight. Dad would never have done a thing like that. But it's still my fault – isn't it? – that people believe he had a motive.'

'You're going to have to curb this instinct to take everything on your own shoulders,' Antony told him seriously, and did not think as he spoke that he was the last person who should be giving such advice.

This time Jamie took a good swig of his ginger ale as though he were thirsty. 'I hadn't really thought about it like that, Mr Maitland,' he said. 'You must be thinking me horrible, as if I don't care at all what happened to Mother. It isn't that, I do care . . . horribly. Though she'd changed, I didn't realise before that people could change like that, and she and Mr Eardley said such dreadful things to me about Dad . . . I think I must have got thoroughly mixed up.'

'Suppose you tell me about it. Would that help?'

'I think perhaps it might.' Again there was that long, appraising look. 'You see, Mr Maitland, I was awfully young when they stopped living together, and though Mother's told me since that they both tried to explain at the time I didn't really realise till later that Dad wasn't just away on a job but that he was never going to live with us again. And when I did . . . well I didn't like it, of course, because I loved them both, but I know that grown-ups are different and this was something I couldn't understand just yet. There was no question of my taking sides between them. But for so long there had been Mother and me, and Dad's visits, not every week but almost, and it all began to seem quite natural.'

Was it fair to take advantage of this situation that had arisen even though it was none of his making? 'I wonder, Jamie, if you can tell me anything about your mother's friends,' Maitland asked.

'Just the neighbours mainly. Mrs Lawson next door and people like that. I know when they were quarrelling, I couldn't help hearing they were shouting so loud, Mother told Dad she'd lost all her friends after he left her. It surprised me because I'd always thought they'd agreed about it together, not that either of them was to blame.'

'I think perhaps, Jamie, it was just that your mother was angry when she said that. You know, I'm sure, that when you lose your temper you don't always say exactly what you mean.'

'Yes, I see. I think I see. Anyway, there was the Bridge Club, Mother would go there every Wednesday afternoon. And friends would come in in the evenings; she enjoyed playing cards more than anything I think. She even tried to teach me, so that I could make a fourth when they needed one, but I don't really like indoor games at all. Except chess, but I have to play that by myself. And then there was some visiting to and fro with people from chapel, but nobody really close. That's what you want to know, isn't it, Mr Maitland? Nobody could have wanted her dead unless they were really close enough to care if she did something they didn't like.'

'I think you're right about that, Jamie. You can't think of anyone?'

'No, no I can't!'

'I shouldn't have asked you that.' The waiter came back then with their order, which they had placed when he brought the drinks, and there was a brief pause until he had gone again. Maitland was wondering whether the boy had talked for long enough to ease the self-imposed burden he had been carrying, but as he picked up his knife and fork Jamie looked directly at him and spoke again.

'You see, Mr Maitland, that day I told you about, Dad explained things to me, and he told me about . . . Mary. I think I would much rather have had her as a stepmother, than Mr Eardley as a stepfather. And now it's dreadfully difficult because I don't know what's going to happen.'

'You have your aunt looking after you now, and another uncle and aunt I believe living here in town.'

'Yes.' This came out rather doubtfully. 'Aunt Amanda is very good to me, I wouldn't want you to think she makes me unhappy. I'm very grateful for what she's doing, giving up her job and everything to look after me. And Uncle Henry has told me I can always have a home with them, and Aunt Maria has said often in the past that she wishes they had a little boy like me. She's rather soppy, you see, Mr Maitland, and sometimes awfully silly, but all the same I realise I ought to be grateful.'

'I don't know about you, Jamie, but I always find that when I get to the stage of having to count my blessings it's a pretty depressing business.'

'Do you feel that too, Mr Maitland?'

77

'Yes, I do. All the same, what you've got to remember now is that your father thinks the world of you, and whatever happens you've got your belief in him to hold on to.'

'Whatever happens?' echoed Jamie rather drearily.

'Yes, because you're too old for me to try to deceive you. I can't promise you a happy ending, in real life they don't come ready-made. So hold on to what you've got, what you can be sure of. You're enough of a man to do that, aren't you?'

'I don't know. I'll try.'

'And in the meantime eat your lunch. Your aunt won't thank me for taking a skeleton back to her.'

To his surprise Jamie giggled at that, sounding suddenly very young. 'She says I've shot up since she last saw me,' he remarked between mouthfuls. 'Did you grow in – in leaps and bounds when you were a boy, Mr Maitland?'

'I expect I did.' But he didn't attempt to elaborate or to ask any more questions, and they ate in silence for a while. Presently Jamie pushed back his plate and sat back.

'Thank you,' he said, 'I enjoyed that very much. Will you tell me what you mean to do now?'

'So long as you promise not to expect too much of me.'

'Tony says –'

'Yes, Tony and his father and mother are friends of mine. He's probably got an exaggerated idea of what it's possible for me to do.'

'All right then, I promise.'

'I shall try to find out a little more about your mother's friends, more than you can tell me. And don't say, Jamie, that a friend wouldn't have done this to her, because it must have been somebody she knew who made the arrangements. Somebody who knew her habits. But as I told you, there's not very much I can do here in Arkenshaw. I shall make a trip down to London again and see if I can find anything more about the man who actually shot your mother.'

'I've seen pictures of him in the paper. There are two things that puzzle me more than anything else, Mr Maitland. One is, why should anyone want to hurt her? I

78

said she'd changed, but I don't think anybody else would have noticed it except me. And the other thing is, if someone wanted to arrange a thing like that how on earth would they know who to ask?'

'You've put your finger right on the two most difficult questions,' Antony told him. 'If I knew the answers we'd have nothing more to worry about.' (Or would we?) 'You've never seen anybody like this man Porson before?'

'No, I'm quite sure of that. With that scar I couldn't have forgotten. But ... can I tell you something else, Mr Maitland?'

'Anything you like, Jamie.'

'It doesn't show me in a very good light,' said Jamie, suddenly grown-up again. 'When I was told what had happened there was just one instant before I started feeling how dreadful it was, and how much I should miss Mother, when the only thing that came to my mind was that now she wouldn't marry Mr Eardley.'

'If you can control your thoughts you're a better man than the rest of us,' Antony assured him.

'You don't think it was very dreadful of me?'

'I don't think it was dreadful at all.'

'You see,' Jamie confided, 'I can't talk about these things to Aunt Amanda, after all she was Mother's sister and loved her very much. Nothing was ever the same after *he* started coming to the house.'

'Where did they meet, do you know?'

'I think at the Bridge Club. Or perhaps at someone's house where he was playing cards too. Mother used to take a job when the sales were on during January and July, and she worked one day a week at the hospital the rest of the year. Of course, there were things she liked to watch on the telly, and she read quite a lot of romances ... awful drivel I thought. But mostly it was bridge that was her main interest.'

'Mr Eardley didn't object to cards?'

'He can't have, can he?'

'And how long had he been coming to the house?'

79

'About two months, I suppose. I don't remember exactly. I didn't like him from the first, I suppose you could really say I didn't try to like him. And that was when Mother began to change, to become more strict with me. But it wasn't until after she told me they were going to be married that she said I mustn't see Dad again. And that was ... absolutely devastating,' said Jamie, obviously rather pleased at having found the *mot juste*. 'And going to chapel with Mother was bad enough, but those Levellers! Mr Eardley tried to tell me I should be ashamed of Dad, because of the kind of life he led. He said that to go to the theatre at all was a sin, or even to go to the pictures. So being an actor put you quite beyond redemption.'

'I'd forget all about that if I were you, Jamie. My wife and I have two very close friends at home in London, and Meg is an actress. You couldn't find a better person anywhere, and I mean that in any sense you like to give to the word.'

'I'll remember that.'

'Yes, I think that would be a very good idea. One last thing, Jamie, how does your Aunt Amanda feel about all this?'

'She was Mother's sister. Of course she's horrified.'

'I didn't mean that exactly. I meant, how does she now feel about your father, has she any ideas of an alternative suspect?'

'She never talks about it at all. And when I try to she says we must just wait and see what happens. But she *is* very kind,' said Jamie again.

'I'm glad of that at any rate.' He looked round and signalled to the waiter. 'Before we go I think you'd better have a dessert of some kind while I have coffee. We can't have you outgrowing your strength.'

III

Oddly enough they reached Jamie's home at almost exactly the hour Maitland had predicted. It was a larger house than he had expected, with quite extensive grounds and a building that must have been the garage tucked away in the trees at the side. Again he thought Amanda must have been watching for them – the door was flung open before he had time to knock. 'So here you are, you horrible boy,' said Amanda to Jamie. At least he wouldn't be able to accuse her of soppiness, Antony thought. 'I put your book in the kitchen, and the chess men are in the cupboard, so you can run along now and leave Mr Maitland and me to talk since that's what he wants.' Jamie departed obediently and she turned to Antony, smiling. 'Forgive me, Mr Maitland, I'm not very used to children but I thought I'd better organise him first. I can't think how I can help you but I'd like to if I can.'

She led the way to a comfortable sitting room, a room that looked lived in, which Maitland found a recommendation, and where a bright fire was burning in the grate. She sat down herself with her back to the window and waved him into the chair opposite her. 'I wouldn't have let Jamie worry you if I'd known what he was up to,' she said. 'But the poor kid doesn't know whether he's coming or going, it may have done him some good to talk to a stranger.'

'I think the important thing is that he should keep his faith in his father,' said Antony.

'Whatever happens?' she challenged him. Amanda Hargreaves was about five foot four, he judged, and still slender though probably in her late thirties. She had a round, smiling face, brown eyes and dark wavy hair that was cut short so that it formed a neat cap over a well-shaped head. Antony looked back at her seriously, weighing his words before he spoke.

'Whatever happens,' he echoed, then. And added deliberately, 'I've never believed in overthrowing idols.'

'I wonder what exactly you mean by that,' she said. 'Are you telling me that you believe in my brother-in-law's innocence?'

'At the moment, Miss Hargreaves, I neither believe nor disbelieve. In any case, as I've just been explaining to your

81

nephew, that isn't my function.'

'I suppose not. You explained it to him, you said, very carefully I've no doubt, so as to convey the impression that your own trust in Richard's innocence was complete.'

'Do you see any harm in that?'

'No, not if you could get away with it. The best I've been able to do is refrain from discussing the matter with Jamie altogether. Poor kid, I don't want to hurt him, and I don't even feel any particular malice towards Richard, though I suppose I should. Because anyone who could arrange matters in such a heartless way . . . poor Laura, she was such a darling.'

'Tell me about your sister.'

'She was three years younger than I am. I can show you her photograph if you like, it's one she sent me years ago and I got my room-mate in Northdean to send it to me because I thought Jamie might like to have it now.' She crossed the room as she spoke and came back with a framed photograph that had been standing on a side table. 'That's Laura,' she said.

Laura Willard might have been three years younger than her sister but the resemblance between them was very marked, almost as marked as that between Richard and his son. A gentle person, Richard had called Amanda, though Antony was getting the feeling that she had a rather more definite personality than that description implied. But on looks alone it might very well have fitted Laura. 'Did you know Lionel Eardley?' Maitland asked abruptly, handing the photograph back without comment.

'No, I didn't. It was to meet him that I took this rather out of season holiday. Laura wrote to me just before the end of November that she'd met this wonderful man and she was going to divorce Richard and get married again. Yes, that's how she put it; she sounded as excited as a schoolgirl. So that's why I was coming to stay.'

'At her suggestion?'

'No, except in the sense that I had a standing invitation to come whenever I liked. But naturally I was curious. And then to arrive . . . well you can imagine how I felt.' Her voice quavered a little but she went on with determined calmness. 'But I'm glad I came, because otherwise what would have happened to Jamie? I think I was able to help him a little, if only because Laura's death made us both so unhappy.'

'And since you took over the care of him?'

'Richard came, of course, as soon as he heard what had happened, and he agreed with me that it was best for Jamie to stay here in his own home for the present. He told me that he too would be getting married, and he talked quite as if . . . well, quite as if there was no question about his being free to do so and make a home for Jamie that way.'

'Did you have any doubts about that at the time?'

'I was so confused and unhappy I don't think I thought about anything clearly, except helping Jamie as much as I could. It was only after Lionel had been here – Lionel Eardley, that is – that I heard about the dreadful quarrels Richard and Laura had had, and I – you can't blame me, can you? – began to wonder.'

'And now you've quite made up your mind?'

'I don't want to think ill of Richard, Mr Eardley,' she protested, 'but in the circumstances what else can I think? It isn't as if anyone else had any reason for wanting Laura dead.'

'I see. You say you've met Eardley.'

'Yes. He came here the day after – luckily Richard wasn't here at the time. And once or twice since to see if there's anything he could do for me. That was natural, wasn't it?'

'Quite natural. What do you think of him?'

'A nice man, a good man. And if his religious beliefs aren't perfectly orthodox, what has that to do with anybody else?' she added defiantly. 'I could quite understand Laura falling in love with him and feeling into the bargain that here was somebody she could trust to look after her.'

'And Jamie.'

'Jamie's very like his father you know, in character as well as in looks.'

'I'm afraid I don't know exactly what you mean by that, Miss Hargreaves.'

'He's determined to go his own way, which may not be the best thing for him. He seems to have taken a dislike to Lionel, but that would have all blown over in time. Which brings me to a question of my own, Mr Maitland. Why did Jamie want to see you?'

'For reassurance, I think, on two points. Because he felt he was to blame for what happened, because he told his father quite clearly how he felt about his mother's proposed marriage. And to make quite sure I didn't give up on the case without even trying.'

'Do you mean Jamie thought that if you explained to the court why Richard had done it it would have made matters better for him?'

'I don't suppose his thought processes were quite as clear as that, Miss Hargreaves. In any case, it wouldn't help. Not in a matter so very obviously premeditated.'

'I see. What did you tell him then?'

'That there were a number of people I wanted to see before I decided on the best line to take in court. And I didn't do anything to disabuse him of the idea that Willard is innocent.'

'But you said . . . did you tell him that's what you believe?'

'He inferred it from something I said. To be frank with you, Miss Hargreaves, that's something I haven't made up my mind about, but I wasn't going to tell Jamie that.'

'You don't think then that it's best to face the facts? Even for someone as young as Jamie.'

'In this case, no. It may, of course be necessary for him to face the fact of his father's conviction.'

'But if Richard . . . it's too horrible to think about, but if he went about it in such a calculated way . . . even if he goes to prison it won't be forever, and for Jamie to be under his influence when he comes out –'

'I think it would be too cruel for Jamie to grow up

believing his father to be a murderer.'

'Better for him to believe in injustice?' said Amanda rather bitterly.

'In this case I think it would,' said Maitland rather sombrely. 'Believe me, Miss Hargreaves, I sympathise with your feelings. Your sister's been killed in a particularly horrible way and like Lionel Eardley you want someone to suffer for it. But we've none of us the right to take it for granted –'

'I'm not really a vindictive person,' said Amanda.

'No, I'm sure you're not. Have you told Jamie what you think about this?'

'No, of course not, not in so many words. But I suppose I've avoided the subject, and he's quite bright enough to realise . . . oh well, if you really think it's best I'll keep my thoughts to myself.'

'Thank you. Has Jamie talked to you about his mother's engagement?'

'No, he hasn't said a word – only, when Lionel has come to the house he's just disappeared.'

'Then, did Eardley talk about Jamie's attitude at all?'

'I suppose you're wondering whether or not he was aware of it. But Laura had told him about it, and he was present once – no, twice I think – when she was quarrelling with Richard. I suppose I must admit Lionel's views are a little out of tune with today. He thought the theatre was wicked, and that anyone connected with it must be contaminated too.'

'He didn't object to cards though? Jamie said –'

'So long as it wasn't for money. And he told me it would be necessary to keep a very close eye on Jamie, in case he had inherited any of his father's tendency towards what he called loose living.'

'But you still feel that Jamie would have got used to the new regime?'

'Yes, I think so, but I do agree that he was still feeling rebellious, and as Richard was so attached to him –'

She left the sentence there, and after a moment Maitland spoke again. 'Wasn't that natural too?'

'I suppose so, but I always thought there was a bit of masculine pride mixed up in it. I'm talking about a number of years ago now, while he and Laura were still together. But about Lionel . . . his views may be a little out of date, but don't you think that's better than being too much the other way?'

'I think there might be two points of view about that,' said Antony. 'Not everyone can be fitted into the same mould. But to return to your sister. Willard tells me they'd never quarrelled, even over the separation, until she told him the first Sunday in December that she wanted a divorce.'

'I don't know that for certain but I can quite well believe it. Laura wasn't at all a quarrelsome person.'

'What about her friends –?'

'I know some of them, of course, because I've always come over regularly for long weekends, and at least one week of my holidays. But I don't think there was anybody she felt really close to. She said once that married couples didn't want to be bothered with a single woman. I think she felt rather let down after Richard left her by some of the people they'd known. This is only an impression, I couldn't swear to it, but I felt she didn't trust anyone very readily after that, so that she didn't want to form any very intimate relatonships.'

'She was going to re-marry,' Antony pointed out.

'That's different, isn't it? Falling in love.'

'I suppose it is. But you have a brother and sister-in-law living here in Arkenshaw?'

'You're wondering why I took it on myself to look after Jamie. They offered to take him of course, but I don't feel Maria would have been the best person in the world for him, particularly not at first. Not that I'm not very fond of her, she's a sentimental soul, and I think she'd have encouraged him to wallow in self-pity, which would not have been the best thing in the world.'

'But if Willard is convicted, and unless I've misunderstood you I think that's what you're expecting, what about your job? If Willard isn't working . . . I don't know his exact financial position, but I don't suppose there'll be very much to spare for Jamie's maintenance.'

'Henry and I have talked about that without coming to any firm decision. Richard had some money from his parents, but I think most of that went on buying this house.'

'Is it in his name or your sister's?'

'In their joint names, I think, so I suppose it could only be sold with his permission. Henry and Maria would like to have Jamie to live with them, and if they decide to make a fight of it – I should say, if Maria does – I daresay they'll get their way. But Henry has promised to assume financial responsibility even if Jamie stays with me, which I think is what Richard would prefer. And I can go back to my job at any time, something new here or back to Northdean, and Jamie is quite old enough to look after himself for an hour or two before I get home from work. Maria, of course, would say that a family atmosphere would be better for him.'

'Have they children?'

'No, I meant a married couple, rather than a single person like myself.'

'What does your brother do, Miss Hargreaves?'

'Didn't Richard tell you? He's a doctor.'

'It didn't come up,' said Antony getting to his feet. 'Well, I've taken up enough of your time, and perhaps your brother and sister-in-law will be able to give me more help on the question of Laura's friends.'

Following his example she was on her feet too. 'Why is that so important?' she asked.

'Because whoever arranged for her death wasn't a stranger to her.'

'I believe you've made up your mind that Richard didn't do it.'

'I think I've already said more than I should on the subject,' Antony told her. 'I'm going back into town now, would you like me to take Jamie with me and leave him at the

87

Conways so that he can spend a little time with his friend, Tony?'

'No, I think he's done enough wandering for today. You needn't worry, I'm not going to scold him, but, for some reason, at the moment I feel he's best under my eye.'

'That's very understanding of you. I hope you don't think, Miss Hargreaves, that my concern for my client's affairs prevents me from feeling a proper sympathy over Mrs Willard's death. It must have been a shock to all her family, and especially perhaps to you.'

'Well you see, I was expecting an especially happy time, knowing how she felt about Lionel. And then to be plunged into mourning instead of into a sort of celebration . . . it was very difficult, I admit.'

'May I go into the kitchen and say goodbye to Jamie?'

'Of course you may.'

Jamie was engaged with a gigantic jigsaw puzzle. He made his farewells politely, but succeeded in conveying the impression that he and the departing visitor shared some not-too-unpleasant secret. 'You do realise, don't you, that he's relying on you now?' said Amanda rather quizzically as she escorted Antony to the front door.

For a moment Maitland's look was startled, then he said with an attempt at lightness, 'I hope he can.' But he repeated to himself as he walked down the road towards the bus stop, for the moment unconscious of the cold and the day and the bitter wind that was blowing, 'I hope to God he can.'

IV

He had barely got back to his room at the hotel when the phone rang to announce that Mr Conway was waiting for him. He went downstairs in a hurry, and he and Chris walked the short distance to the station yard, where again the car was parked with perfect legality. 'You'll forgive me for saying so,' said Chris, when they were halted by the red light at the first set of traffic signals they encountered, 'but you look rather like a cat with its fur rubbed the wrong way.'

'Is it so noticeable?' Antony laughed. 'I suppose I may as well tell you now as later, I'm staying! At least until I've seen the few people I can see with propriety; after that I think I'd be more useful in London. There may be something to be gathered about Porson's associates there.'

'That, of course,' said Chris philosophically, 'was obvious from the beginning. That you intended to go into the matter a bit further, I mean.'

'Well, don't ask me if I've made up my mind, that's all. I'd give a good deal for a really sound conviction as to Willard's guilt or innocence. But I'd better tell you what's been happening to me since you dropped me off for lunch.'

'You've been thinking,' Chris hazarded.

'I haven't really had time to think.' He went on to describe Jamie's advent, their talk over lunch, and his visit to Amanda Hargreaves. 'Neither talk was particularly illuminating,' he concluded, 'but it's obvious I've got to give Willard the benefit of the doubt.'

'You know what I feel about it, I'm glad you're staying.'

'You and Star,' said Antony. 'I think perhaps it was Star's opinion more than anything else that tipped the scales. She's a very level-headed person and I have great faith in her judgement.'

'She married me,' said Chris rather smugly. 'But I don't know if I quite like your dismissing my own opinion as negligible.'

Antony grinned. 'I don't,' he assured him. 'But I do think you may subconsciously be influenced more than Star is by the desire to prove yourself right and Inspector Duckett wrong.'

Chris was slowing for the turn that meant they were getting near their destination. 'What the hell do you mean by that?' he inquired without heat.

'Just that Star, I'm sure, is quite confident that whatever happens her father will forgive her for differing from his opinion. I don't suppose you feel quite the same confidence.'

Chris thought about that for a moment. 'You may be right,' he said cautiously. 'But it's deeper than that with my revered father-in-law. He wouldn't mind if it was only a matter of my disagreeing with his opinion, it's because of Jim Ryder's death that he feels so bitter about it.'

'Yes, I can understand that. To have a colleague killed in the course of duty . . . I feel badly about it myself, worse than about Laura Willard's death, because after all I got to know Constable Ryder pretty well. But you do realise – don't you, Chris? – that if Willard is innocent we're going to have the devil's own job to prove it.'

'That,' said Chris, pulling into the side of the road and stopping close to the high wall that bounded the Arkenshaw Waterworks property, 'is exactly why I screamed for help to you.'

Old Peel Farm, where Star's father and grandmother lived, stood on high ground on the outskirts of the town with the newly-made golf course behind it. Not all that newly made, Antony reflected, as they got out of the car and faced the wind that was even more challenging here. It was just that he remembered the place before it had been constructed. In the sunshine the stone house could look mellow and friendly, yet today Antony felt it looked almost as bleak and forbidding as the prison had done. But inside there would be warmth and friendliness . . . and Grandma Duckett, who appealed irresistibly to his sense of the ridiculous and for whom he entertained a very real affection. If he had been in the habit of dissecting his own motives he would have realised that for him the two things very often went together, and would have put it down no doubt to some defect in his own character. As it was he merely found the thought of the meeting pleasurable and looked forward to it with simple satisfaction.

He let Chris precede him up the flagged path to the front door and ply the knocker. The thought occurred to Antony as his friend did so that probably having a bell would come

90

under Grandma Duckett's disapproval as 'wasting the electric'. Far better, obviously, to make use of energy provided by those who sought admission. There was a little delay before the door opened, which probably meant the Inspector was out and the old lady was having to make her difficult way to the door herself. And sure enough there she was, looking from one to the other of them and saying rather grudgingly, 'Don't stand about there, come in and shut door.' Letting in a draught was obviously an equally blameworthy form of wastage.

But after knowing her so long Antony had certainly not expected anything effusive in Grandma's greeting, and already his spirits were beginning to lighten imperceptibly. When they had followed her into the kitchen, which was really more of a living room, there was a bright fire in the grate and tea things set out on a small table pulled close to her favourite Windsor chair, which in its way was welcome enough. 'You'd best sit down,' she said to Antony. 'You look starved, both of you,' (which was only her way of remarking on the cold) 'so we'll have some tea right away.'

That was Chris's cue to disappear into the scullery, from which they heard the sound of running water, and reappear a moment later with a large black kettle, which was far too heavy nowadays for Grandma to lift. As long as Antony had known her her hands had been twisted with arthritis, but though she must be well into her eighties now she had really changed very little. A stiff-backed, stout old lady, with a roseleaf complexion and creamy-white hair drawn into a tight bun. Her eyes were a very vivid blue and the direct way he had of looking at you matched the forthrightness of her speech. Antony waited until she had settled herself, kissed her cheek lightly, and then went to his favourite place, perched on a sort of pouffe at the other side of the old-fashioned range. 'How's Jenny, then?' she asked him.

'Very well. She sent you her love.'

He was relaxing already as he always did in Grandma's presence, and the thought struck him, not for the first time,

91

that it was amusing how she would accord Jenny the familiarity of her Christian name, while he had remained Mr Maitland for all these years. Perhaps it was because their very first meeting had been in the course of his profession.

'She didn't want you to come here, I've no doubt.'

'She knows I have to come away on business sometimes.'

'A good girl, that one,' said Grandma Duckett flatly, which to her was the equivalent of the most effusive praise. She smiled rather grimly as she spoke, so that for the first time Antony realised who it was that Vera had reminded him of when he met her; or rather, as she herself would have reminded him, when she had pursued him down the steps of the Shire Hall in Chedcombe to ask his help all those years ago. But he was missing Jenny, as he always did when they were apart, and if he voiced his agreement he would probably become maudlin himself, so he asked instead,

'Chris said Tommy isn't at home at the moment. How is he?'

'Over to Bradford University,' said Grandma proudly. Tommy Ridealgh had been a client of Antony's five years before at the tender age of thirteen, and on his release (without a stain on his character as Grandma put it) the Ducketts had given him a home. 'As to his health he's never been one to ail aught, but I was that pleased he got his entrance without any trouble, he's a clever lad.'

'What is he studying?' asked Maitland, concealing his surprise, not at Tommy's alleged intelligence, about which he was in no doubt, but about his present location.

'Now, don't tell me he never told you,' said Grandma, eyeing Chris, who was now spooning tea into the pot that was keeping warm on top of the range, with some severity. 'Tommy never gave up that idea he had as a lad of going to sea, and as he's of a practical turn of mind it seemed best for him to study engineering. So that's what –'

'Grandma!' said Chris, looking up from his task for a moment.

'What can't be spoken of in the daylight,' said Grandma

didactically, 'didn't ought to be done at all. I know what Sir Nicholas said, and in a way he's right. *Let not thy right hand know what thy left hand doeth.* But there's no call to keep Mr Maitland in the dark,' she concluded, and if this last statement contained a contradiction of what she had said before, neither of her hearers would have dreamed of pointing it out.

Antony grinned openly. 'Uncle Nick?' he said. 'The old fraud! You mean to tell me he's paying for Tommy's education?'

'Wrote to Fred two years ago, he did, to find out where Tommy was aiming. Goodness of heart, I call it, and no cause for you to be laughing at him, Mr Maitland, when you did ought to know better.'

'It's just . . . well if you heard the lectures he reads me about getting involved with my clients,' said Antony, 'you'd see what I mean. *Be sure you sins will find you out,*' he added, feeling perhaps that the quotation might soften Grandma, but she only scowled at him. 'Well, I've no need to ask how you are,' he added, still with pacific intent. 'You're looking as bonny as ever –'

'None of your nonsense now!'

'– and I saw Star last night, so there's just the Inspector to inquire after.'

Chris by now had finished his task and was sitting down waiting for the kettle to boil. He gave Antony a reproachful look, as though he deplored the introduction of a dangerous subject. 'He's well enough,' said Grandma. 'You've heard about Jim Ryder, though?'

'I have indeed, and I'm more than sorry –'

'Being sorry won't mend matters,' the old lady told him with some truth. 'Our Star tells me that actor friend of theirs wouldn't have done it, wouldn't have arranged for his wife to be killed which is a piece of wickedness that led to Jim getting himself killed. But I don't know, girls can get led astray by a handsome face.'

'Come now, Grandma, she married Chris!' said Antony

irrepressibly, and was answered with a dark look.

'Pisces!' said Grandma making it sound to Antony's irreverent mind like a swear word. 'Not that it's turned out so badly, what with young Tony and all. And you're right of course, our Star has sense enough not to marry for looks' – Antony exchanged an apologetic look with Chris – 'but it might make her over-ready to believe him, this Mr Willard being an actor and all.'

'Chris believes him too,' Antony ventured.

'Oh him! Everyone knows that Pisces folk are apt to let their imagination run away with them,' said Grandma. 'Capricorn, which is Star's sign, as well you know . . . that's different. And I'd like you to tell me what you think about it, Mr Maitland.' From which he inferred that Grandma was not quite so scornful of Star's opinion as she maintained.

'Is a person with my birth sign any more likely to be right?' asked Antony, teasing her.

'Cancer,' said Grandma thoughtfully, 'with Mercury in the ascendant. Mercury's intellectual, he is, which ought to help, but you're ruled by the moon, I've told you that before, and intuition isn't always a good guide.'

'Uncle Nick just calls it guessing,' said Antony apologetically.

'That's what I mean, isn't it? And from the look of you,' she added, 'you're at it again and worrying about it. Let that stand for a minute to draw,' she broke off to instruct Chris, who had got up quietly to fill the teapot. As well as he knew her by now Antony had never yet summoned up the courage to tell her that he really didn't like Sergeant-Major's tea.

Chris didn't answer her directly, though he put the pot down as directed and resumed his seat. 'Antony's going to look into the matter a little,' he said, 'though I don't think it gives him much scope for inquiry.'

'I might have known it. Does that mean you've made up your mind?' she demanded of Maitland.

'I wish I had,' said Antony with feeling.

'*The spirit within me constraineth me*,' said Grandma, falling

94

back on the Bible as she so often did when she forgot about the signs of the Zodiac.

'It isn't just that I have no right to judge him when he says he's innocent,' said Antony, taking her meaning well enough. 'There's his son to consider too – Jamie.'

'What's the boy got to do with it, except that from what Fred's told me he's the reason they quarrelled?'

'Tell me something, Grandma. Even supposing Willard is guilty, don't you think it would be better for Jamie to believe his father was the victim of injustice, rather than that he was a murderer?'

'Truth will out,' said Grandma.

'Yes, *I* want to know the truth, but if it's unpleasant I don't see any point in ramming it down Jamie's throat.'

''appen you're right,' said Grandma thoughtfully.

'You're not just humouring me?' asked Antony suspiciously.

'Nay, you'll have to make up your own mind about that,' said Grandma. 'But you're worried, which is daft-like. You've got your job to do and that's all there is to it.'

'I wonder.' Chris got up quietly and poured the tea, and Antony, who preferred the black brew that Grandma insisted on scalding hot rather than when it had cooled a little picked up his cup. 'You see, Grandma,' he said, speaking for the moment as though they were alone, 'Chris and Star are so sure and I like Willard myself. Even apart from Jamie's feelings I want to believe him.'

'Don't take on so, lad. As long as you know there's a danger that might influence you there'll be no harm done.'

'I wish I was sure of that. Can you tell me anything about Laura Willard's family, Grandma? I often tell Chris he knows everything about Arkenshaw, but there are times when you've been able to put both of us right.'

'It's a small town compared with London,' said Grandma, 'but you can't expect Chris to know things that went on before he was born. All the same I don't see how it'll help you.'

'If Willard didn't do it –'

'What sign was he born under?' asked Grandma.

'I don't know. But . . . didn't you tell me, Chris?'

'His birthday's somewhere at the beginning of November. You asked me that before, Grandma.'

She ignored the reminder. 'Scorpio,' she said reflectively. 'An actor . . . I might have known it, I suppose. But there'll be a darker side to him too, passionate,' she went on, disliking the word. 'And I'll tell you something else about Scorpio. They're saints or sinners, there's no half way with them.'

Maitland thought about that for a moment. 'Should I take comfort from that?' he asked, amusement tinging his voice again for a moment. 'But I was going to say, if he's innocent someone else is guilty, and it wasn't someone who was a stranger to Laura. The family came from Arkenshaw, I believe, and I thought perhaps Henry Hargreaves could tell me something about her friends. I asked her sister Amanda but she's been away . . . how long has she been away, Grandma?'

'Ten or eleven years, I think.'

'As long as that? Well, that would explain why she doesn't know much about Laura's present friends.'

'You know, Mr Maitland, I don't approve of idle talk.'

'I'm asking you only for the barest outline . . . so that I don't put my foot in it when I talk to Henry and his wife,' said Antony rather less than honestly.

It seemed, however, that the explanation passed muster, or Grandma had her own reasons for deciding to treat it as if it did. 'I daresay Chris's father could tell you more about Henry Hargreaves than I can, being as he's a doctor too.'

'Dad doesn't know him, except by sight,' Chris put in.

'A younger man than Dr Conway, of course,' Grandma went on, 'though older than his sisters. A conscientious man so I've been told, and married to a wife who backs him up in every way.'

'I was told she was sentimental,' said Antony.

'Well, if you think that's a sin –'

'Certainly not,' he told her hastily.

'It's true enough, I suppose,' said Grandma, frowning frightfully as though it was important to get the matter completely clear in her own mind. 'They haven't any children, and I've been told it's been a great grief to them. And not just because Henry's mother blames it on Maria.'

'Henry's mother?' asked Antony, immediately alert. 'Is she still alive?'

'And why not, may I ask? A good fifteen years younger than me . . . well perhaps not quite as much as that. But no reason to be dying now – poor woman – if it weren't that she's got cancer.'

'You speak as if you knew her, Grandma.'

'Of course I do. Goes to chapel regularly, she does, at least until she got ill.'

'Is her husband living too?'

'Nay, he died years ago. Not long after Laura was married, or perhaps a year or two later. I don't remember exactly, but it was after Amanda left Arkenshaw. He was manager of the local branch of Bramley's Bank,' she added for good measure, 'and a warm man by all accounts, which means the boy will be wealthy one of these days.'

'Henry?' asked Antony, rather bewildered by the description.

'Nay, not Henry. This Jamie you're so worried about.'

'I don't quite see, I'm afraid.'

Grandma seemed to be debating with herself so that Antony thought, amused again, that she was wondering whether to speak any further would come under the heading of scurrilous talk or not. 'I told you Susan Hargreaves was a good, God-fearing woman,' she said at last. 'And that's true enough, but there's no denying that once she's gotten an idea into her head there's nothing on this earth can get it out again.'

'Are you trying to tell me she quarrelled with her family?'

'Not to say quarrelled, that wouldn't have suited her

97

notions at all. But when they were what she considered wayward she wasn't going to reward them for it. Amanda never married, though there were one or two lads after her when she was younger. That didn't please her mother, and then there was the question of her going away when Arkenshaw was good enough for the rest of the family and should have been good enough for her. I'm telling you what Susan said to me more than once. And Henry married a woman who was barren it seemed, though how he was expected to know that beforehand I can't imagine.' Antony and Chris exchanged a glance again, which didn't go unremarked. 'Don't you go talking to me about trial marriages,' said Grandma severely, and added, inconsistent again, 'I won't have suchlike mentioned in this house. They were chapel, like our Star, and such a thing would never have occurred to them.'

'I'm sure it wouldn't, Grandma,' said Antony meekly, ignoring the implied slur on his own and Chris's characters. 'I think you're telling me that old Mr Hargreaves left all his money to his wife, but that she cut both Amanda and Henry out of her will for various reasons that seemed good to her.'

'Aye, that's it. And Laura too, think on, though she'd have benefited of course, at least until Jamie was old enough to manage his own money.'

'I . . . see. And Mrs – Susan Hargreaves did you say? –told you this herself. Do you think it was common knowledge?'

'That I can't tell you. There were those as were closer to her; I don't suppose she stopped at telling me. But don't you go getting ideas into your head, Mr Maitland.'

'You mustn't blame me, Grandma, you're putting them there.'

'What daft notion are you getting now?'

'Only that there is nothing in this world that causes so much dissension among families as a dispute over an inheritance.'

'Aye, and you'll be adding in a moment that Henry and his wife would have liked the rearing of Jamie for more

98

reasons than their liking for t'lad.'

'The two things together form quite a formidable indictment . . . don't you think?'

'No, I do not, and I'll thank you not to be putting words into my mouth.' Grandma's cup was empty now and she passed it to Chris for a refill. Her hands must be getting worse, Antony thought irrelevantly. As long as he had known her she'd always needed help with the heavy kettle, but never before had he seen her relinquish charge of the teapot. 'And since you're feeling so clever, Mr Maitland, tell me this. How would an Arkenshaw doctor know where to look for a hired assassin?'

'I don't know, Grandma, but that's a difficulty whoever is the guilty party. How would an actor working mainly in the north of England –?'

'He gets about, doesn't he? And I daresay he knows all sorts of people.' The hint of argument seemed to be hardening Grandma's opinion, at which he shouldn't have been surprised. 'Not that I'm saying he did it,' she said after a moment, relenting a little. 'Only that the Hargreaves are a respectable family, never a word to be said against any of them except for what poor Susan thought up for herself.'

'You said she'd have cut Laura out of her will too.'

'Yes. She was pleased about the marriage, thought this Richard Willard seemed a nice young fellow, but of course when they separated . . . well, she had her grandson to concentrate on, so I expect that made it easier for her to disapprove of the others.'

'Were they a united family, apart from Mrs Susan Hargreaves's attitude I mean?'

'I never heard owt to the contrary.'

'I see,' said Antony again, a little less doubtfully this time. Better not push Grandma too far, she was probably already regretting having told him so much. 'Is it too much to hope that you know something about Lionel Eardley too?'

'Oh him! One of these Levellers, as if going to chapel like a Christian isn't good enough for them.'

99

'I'm sure he thinks of himself as a Christian.'

'*For God shall bring every work into judgement, with every secret thing, whether it be good, or whether it be evil,*' said Grandma rather obscurely.

'Be that as it may,' said Antony, not feeling himself qualified to comment, 'I gather he considers himself a righteous man.'

'That's as may be. Young Tommy's told me a thing or two about those Levellers. Heaven help the boy, that's all I say, if Lionel Eardley had had the bringing up of him. Not that I'm condemning wickedness, mind you. *He that diggeth a pit shall fall into it.*'

'If you mean Richard Willard, suppose the pit wasn't of his digging.' He broke off and gave her his sudden smile. 'If Uncle Nick were here he wouldn't be able to resist remarking that *he that begetteth a fool doeth it to his sorrow.*'

'Well, I'm not saying you're a fool for wondering,' said Grandma surprisingly. 'But it's reet daft to be worrying about t'matter the way I can see you are. *The way of the transgressor is hard*, and there's nowt you or anybody else can do about it.'

'Is Eardley a local man?'

'We weren't talking about Lionel Eardley.'

'No, we got back to Willard, didn't we?' He came to his feet restlessly and stood looking down at her in a troubled way. Chris got up too, quietly stacked the cups on the tray, and disappeared with it into the scullery. 'I quite agree with you, Grandma,' said Antony, 'It's beyond forgiveness to arrange another person's death so cold-bloodedly.'

'Come here,' the old lady ordered him. He went across to her side and she took his left hand in both of hers, and her blue eyes were very serious as she looked up at him. 'Chris told me you'd been having some trouble, back before Christmas.'

'Yes, Grandma, I –'

'No need to go into it all again, Chris told me,' she repeated. 'But he said too that things should be straight

100

going for you now . . . now that you didn't have an enemy in t'police.'

'They will be, Grandma,' he assured her.

She took no notice of that. 'I thought 'appen you'd go a bit easier on yourself from now on,' she said in a scolding tone. 'But I reckon it's not in your nature.'

'Perhaps it isn't,' he said ruefully. 'I only know –'

'That you don't in your heart of hearts believe that this actor chap arranged to have Laura killed,' she finished for him.

'If I could be sure –'

'Act as if you are.' She squeezed his hand, and dropped hers into her lap again. '*Her end is bitter as wormwood, sharp as a two-edged sword.*'

'It wasn't a two-edged sword, it was a high-powered rifle,' said Maitland, trying to inject a little humour into the situation again. 'And whatever Laura had done she didn't deserve to die like that.'

For a moment it seemed as though Grandma were going to add something, but Chris came back into the room and the moment for confidences passed, if indeed, thought Maitland, it hadn't been just his imagination. They talked for a little while of other things before saying goodbye and leaving to go back to Ingleton Crescent.

'Grandma was in even more sybilline mood than usual,' said Antony as they got back into the car, but Chris wasn't having any of that.

'I don't suppose the sybil would have quoted the Bible to you,' he said rather sourly, and seemed disinclined for further conversation as they drove back to town. But Maitland was thinking that when Grandma Duckett forsook her beloved astrology for her almost-equally-beloved Bible (and how did she square the two obsessions in her own mind?) it generally meant she was uneasy about something. He might have pressed his questions, but he didn't think she was ready to tell him . . . yet.

V

When they arrived at the Conways' home Tony's greeting was boisterous and grew even more so when he saw the gift that Jenny had picked out for him. Finally she and Meg had consulted Roger, as the practical member of the foursome, and he had devoted Thursday's lunchtime to helping her pick it out, so that it came with his guarantee that it would keep the boy quiet for hours. Antony's objection, 'So long as he doesn't want my help in assembling it,' had been waved aside and in the event it seemed that the others had been right. Tony retired to a corner of the room and was soon absorbed in some very professional-looking blueprints; the contents of the box his present had come in were spread around him on the floor in a haphazard sort of way.

'Did you see Dad?' Star asked as the others settled themselves comfortably round the fire. And then, recollecting herself, 'I think you ought to give Antony a drink straight away, Chris, even though it is rather early. To take away the taste of Grandma's tea,' she explained.

'That's a very good idea,' Antony agreed in a heartfelt way.

'You really are a coward, you know,' said Star, 'never telling her how you like it.'

'Grandma,' said Antony, with mock seriousness, 'is enough to strike terror into the stoutest heart. And on the whole you know, Star, I think her company's worth it. But to answer your question, no, your father wasn't at home.'

Chris had gone out for a moment, presumably in search of liquid refreshment. 'Did Grandma tell you how he feels about Chris taking on Richard's defence?' Star asked.

'No, she didn't mention that. I expect she realised you'd have told me.'

'Or how she feels about it?' Star insisted.

'Not that either. She certainly displayed no animosity, if that's what you're worrying about. In fact I rather think she sympathises with Chris's dilemma.'

'That's a relief. You see, I do realise that to anyone who doesn't know Richard – and neither of them do – it must seem awfully disloyal to Jim Ryder to be defending the man they think was responsible for his death.'

'There's one thing I don't think you need worry about,' said Maitland, 'however matters turn out. Your father won't go on holding it against you. He's far too fond of you.'

'Even of "that Chris?"' asked Star, smiling.

'You're quoting Grandma there, not your father, and even she hasn't called him that for a long time,' Antony assured her. 'I really think you've nothing to worry about as far as the family's concerned.'

'But about Richard?'

'That's a different matter. Chris put his finger on it when he said that our main difficulty would be Laura's sheer – may I coin a word? – unmurderability. Though I was surprised at the size of the house and grounds, I admit.'

Chris had come back into the room while they were speaking, and now he began to pour the drinks without reference to anyone's taste, which in any case he knew well enough. 'As I understand it Laura was very keen on having a proper home when they married, even though Richard had to be away so much in the very nature of things. And you must remember that twelve or thirteen years ago, whichever it was, property wasn't nearly so expensive as it is today. After they separated Laura still wanted to stay on in the same place, and I expect Richard thought it was the easiest thing to let her have her way. The best thing for Jamie too, on the principle, I suppose, that children are rather like cats and get attached to the places they're used to.'

'Yes, I see. Did Laura drive? I know you mentioned her being on her way to catch the bus when she was shot.'

'She had a little car, I expect it's still in the garage –'

'Which, in keeping with everything else about the place, is big enough for a bus.'

'– but most people use the bus to get around the town,

parking can be so very inconvenient.'

'And the police are rather more vigilant now on the question of keeping to the rules,' Maitland commented. 'It hasn't escaped my notice, Chris, that you're being rather more careful yourself nowadays.'

'Star thinks it looks bad for the son-in-law of an Inspector of Police to keep getting traffic tickets,' said Chris, smiling at his wife. 'Did you get any help from Grandma's talk about the Hargreaves family?'

'Well, no one had mentioned old Mrs Hargreaves before.'

'I'd never heard of her,' said Chris.

'But you must have done, Star?'

'I knew there was a Mrs Hargreaves that Grandma used to be friendly with at chapel, when they were both helping at sales of work or bake sales or things like that. But I never connected her with Richard's wife, I'm afraid. Was she – ?'

'Her mother. It seems she's a lady of some substance . . . or what would you say Grandma meant by the word "warm" in that connection, Chris?'

'Wealthy,' said Chris succinctly, and Star nodded her agreement.

'A wealthy lady then, and Grandma says she's dying of cancer. It would be interesting to know how near to death she is. If she's in the hospital or a nursing home, do you think your father would forget his principles long enough to find that out for us, Chris?'

'Not a hope.'

'No, I thought not. Perhaps Dr Hargreaves will tell me, though on the whole I'd rather find him cagey on the subject.'

'If you're thinking that would be a mark against him, I don't agree with you,' said Chris. 'And do you really think – ?'

'Laura Willard was certainly shot, and I don't suppose Porson did it just because he wanted the practice,' said Antony. 'Somebody wanted her dead, and if it wasn't Willard we'd better start looking for another motive.'

104

'You think you may have found one?'

'I think we've got to consider the possibility. According to Grandma, Star, old Mrs Hargreaves is leaving all her money to Jamie, because of some not-very-valid grievances she has against her own children. Dr Hargreaves and his wife are childless and Jamie referred to his aunt as . . . I think the expression was "soppy". If they're really upset about not having a child of their own, probably one of their own blood – or Henry's blood at least – would be the best substitute. They'd be the natural people to have the care of him, and therefore the spending of his income at least until he comes of age. And if you're going to tell me that's a tenuous argument, Chris, just try thinking of another Lord High Substitute for yourself.'

'I know it's difficult, and I can't for the life of me see how any ordinary citizen would know anything about Porson. He was known to the police, and the local chaps were tipped off when he came here, but even when you remember that a crooked copper's not unknown today Laura doesn't seem to have numbered any among her acquaintance, bent or otherwise.'

'That's a perfectly valid objection, but the same thing can be said about Willard. With the unfortunate difference that he certainly had some conversation with Porson. I'm very much afraid that in considering the matter we're going to have to write off the selection of an assassin as pure chance.'

'All right then, but I still think that fellow Eardley is our best bet,' said Chris stubbornly.

'That's only because you've taken a dislike to him,' Maitland pointed out. 'Give me one good reason –'

'I can't, as you very well know.'

'I'm sure we can think of something,' said Star. 'After all he's forty and never been married before. Perhaps he proposed to Laura on an impulse, and then regretted what he'd done. It may have been the idea of having a stepson, or perhaps when he thought it over he didn't like the idea of marrying a divorced woman after all. Or perhaps she said

105

something that showed him that her principles were not quite as strict as his own. Couldn't you go and see that man – their minister, I can't remember his name – the one you talked to when Tommy was in trouble?'

'No, I don't think so. Think about it, Star,' said Maitland, smiling at her. 'Can you imagine us going to him and saying, Mr Harte – that was his name – without any grounds at all we suspect one of your flock of being a murderer. Can you tell us anything about him to help us prove it?'

Star returned the smile. 'No, I can see that would be difficult,' she agreed. 'All the same I don't think you should forget about this Mr Eardley altogether.'

'I can't. I shall have to cross-examine him when we get into court,' said Antony, 'but meanwhile . . . did Chris explain to you, Star, there isn't very much more I can do here?'

'Are you going back to town tomorrow, then?'

'Perhaps in the evening. I want to see Dr Hargreaves and his wife, but any other inquiries you can put in hand, Chris, and I'll be better occupied talking to Sykes – Superintendent Sykes he is now – in London. I don't suppose he'll be able to tell me anything about Porson that's relevant to the case, but I think I ought to try.'

'Yes, I see that.' Chris had produced a notebook, 'Someone will be seeing Mrs Lawson, the next door neighbour, in case she can give us any lead on Laura's other friends. And of course there are the witnesses from the pub . . . the police slipped up pretty badly there, didn't they? Leaving it to Eardley to root them out.'

'I don't know about that. They knew Porson had gone to The Bishop's Move around lunchtime each Sunday since he'd been in Arkenshaw, but none of them had ever actually followed him into the pub. When they asked questions after Laura's death it was at a time when neither of the two men who seem to have noticed him talking to Willard was present. The landlord had got so used to Porson sitting quietly in a corner and not talking to anyone that he

106

probably didn't observe him very closely. I don't think you can really blame the police.'

'Well, it was the Detective Branch of course,' said Chris, 'but I'm pretty sure it's one of the things that's riling Inspector Duckett. It may not be logical to take it out on us but –'

'Antony thinks Dad'll get over it,' said Star consolingly. 'I'm sure he's right about that.'

'There's just one other thing,' said Maitland before Chris could argue the point. 'There are two flats above the Imperial Café, aren't there? Do you know who lives in them?'

'Yes, I do.' Chris was turning the pages of his notebook, but gave up presently and slipped it back into his pocket again. 'Their names aren't important, there's a man and his wife in one, and a bachelor in the other who seems to do a good deal of entertaining. But none of them, as far as we can find out, had any connection at all with any of the people even remotely concerned with this business, and none of them saw Porson casing the joint, which he or the person who employed him must have done, I suppose, and none of them heard anything when Laura was killed, not even the sound of the shot. Not consciously anyway. The bachelor who has the top flat hadn't got home, the other two had just got in but they were talking and didn't notice anything.'

'Not even Porson hurling himself down the fire escape.'

'Not consciously anyway,' Chris repeated. 'The wife said that if they'd heard anyone they'd have thought it was their neighbour.'

'That's that, then. Did you fix a time for us to visit the Hargreaves, Chris?'

'They'll be in all the afternoon unless he's called out to a patient. I said we'd get there about two-thirty. Is that all right with you?'

'Perfectly all right. I'll book out of the hotel, shall I, and put my case in the car? Then you can take me straight to the station afterwards. There's a train at four thirty-five.'

'Come here to lunch, then,' Star invited. 'It's no good your having to pay for an extra day at the hotel.'

Antony grinned at her. 'I'll come to lunch very willingly,' he assured her, 'though I don't really think the hotel would grudge me an extra couple of hours.'

After that Dr Conway arrived and the talk became general. Maitland thought, as he had done before, that you'd only to look at the father to see what the son would be like in thirty years' time. But the doctor was a man for whom he entertained a very real regard, and as Tony was still locked up in his puzzle the evening passed very pleasantly, and they were free from interruptions even before the youngest member of the party was despatched to bed.

Sunday, 2nd February

I

If Maitland had hoped for a quiet morning until it was time for him to go round to Ingleton Crescent he was to be disappointed. He lingered over breakfast with the Sunday papers, drinking more coffee than was probably good for him, but no sooner had he got back to his room and started packing than the telephone interrupted him. 'There's a Miss Norton to see you, Mr Maitland,' the receptionist's voice announced.

It took him a moment to recognise the name. Mary Norton, of course, whom his client wished to marry. 'Ask her to wait,' he said, 'I'll come straight down.' But as he went he was thinking to himself rather wryly, *My reputation, Iago, my reputation*! For what else could he blame for this damnable habit people seemed to be getting into of approaching him directly, instead of more formally through his instructing solicitor. Not that Jamie would know anything about instructing solicitors . . .

But his ill-humour vanished as soon as he saw his visitor. Mary Norton was standing rather forlornly in the middle of the lobby, watching the lift gates, whereas Maitland, who had been lodged on the first floor, came down one of the rather elegant twin staircases that met on the mezzanine. His first thought was, if that's the girl she doesn't look anything like an actress, which was nonsense because neither did Meg. But Meg's unthinking elegance was only a front, as he knew well enough; and so possibly might Mary Norton's look of being a respectable nonentity be a deliberate camouflage, either habitual or assumed for this one occasion.

When he spoke her name she turned to him eagerly. 'Mr Maitland? It's so very good of you to agree to see me.' And whatever pretence might be involved, whatever sort of an act she might be putting on, he was immediately convinced that her rather imploring look was completely genuine. With no make-up except a dab of powder she wasn't exactly memorable, but her features were regular without being in any way distinguished, and he remembered that Meg had once told him this was a positive asset when it came to making up for some particular part. The colour of her hair was nondescript, dark rather than fair, but her grey eyes were fringed with almost black lashes and added a touch of beauty to her appearance without owing anything to the use of mascara.

He thought afterwards that his answer to her greeting had been to mutter something completely meaningless, but he looked around him quickly and then at his watch and added, 'At this hour there's unlikely to be anybody in the lounge. Come in there, Miss Norton, and then we can talk.' But he added when they were settled near the window in the otherwise deserted room, 'I daresay you don't realise it, but if you've anything to tell me concerning Richard Willard's case you should approach me through Chris Conway.'

'I've read quite a lot of mystery stories,' she said, which was perhaps as good an answer to his query as any other. 'But I've nothing to tell you, Mr Maitland, nothing you could use in court, I mean. But I thought perhaps you'd listen to me and perhaps not – not judge Richard too hardly for any irregularity in our relationship. And besides, there's Jamie.'

'My dear Miss Norton' – Maitland had taken a liking to her on sight, but he wasn't quite ready to relax completely in his attitude towards her – 'it isn't my business to make moral judgements even if I wanted to. Which I can assure you I don't.'

She eyed him searchingly for a moment. 'No, I think you're telling me the truth,' she said. 'But I've heard this and that about you,' (if she noticed the fact that he stiffened as she spoke she made no sign) 'and one thing is that you are very happily married.'

'I am as it happens, but –'

'So I thought perhaps –'

It seemed that the conversation was doomed to continue in a series of half-finished sentences. 'You thought perhaps I'd be apt to confuse Willard's relationship with you with his capacity for planning his wife's death. I don't think that's an error I'm likely to fall into, but I won't disguise it from you, Miss Norton, I can't answer for its effect on the jury.'

'I was afraid of that. The prosecution aren't calling me –'

'No, I knew that, and now I can see why.'

'I don't understand you.'

'You're so obviously not the typical home-wrecker.'

That brought a faint smile. 'And Laura had thrown Richard out four years before we started living together. Doesn't that make a difference?'

'If I can ram the fact home to the jury with sufficient clarity perhaps it will. Tell me about your association with Willard.'

'It's rather difficult now, it all seemed so natural at the time. We worked together in Rothershaw for several seasons, and it was only gradually that we began to realise exactly how much we meant to each other. And when we did . . . what I wanted to emphasise to you, Mr Maitland, is that when we started to live together we made a commitment to each other, just as much as if we were marrying. I'd never met Laura, naturally; Richard was afraid that if he asked her for a divorce she might somehow interfere with his seeing Jamie as often as he was used to. He's very devoted to his son, you know, and in a way I feel I've come to know the boy through hearing Richard talk of him. I couldn't believe that any woman would want to disturb what there was between them, but Richard wasn't so sure and didn't want to take a chance. In a way I have to admit I was pleased when Laura raised the question of divorce, I'd have liked to be married to Richard, and I'd have been very willing to accept Jamie either on a permanent or a temporary basis. But when Richard told me what his wife's attitude was . . . I'm not helping matters by telling you all this, am I, I'm just confirming what the police say was his motive?'

'Don't worry about that for the moment, Miss Norton. We're not in court.'

'I suppose Richard will have to give evidence.'

'He's under no compulsion to do so, but I couldn't advise him against it. That could have a very adverse effect on the jury's opinion of him.'

'Yes, I understand that. But what I was going to say was that I'm telling you no more than he said himself, he'd never lie about his feelings for Jamie, and as far as I can tell the police seem to know all about Laura's attitude towards their meeting in future.'

'That's thanks to the man she wanted to marry, Lionel Eardley.'

'Richard told me about him, but I didn't quite realise –'

'I haven't met him myself because he'll be giving evidence for the prosecution and it would be against legal etiquette for me to talk to him before the trial. But I'm afraid that you can take it that Laura's conversion – if you can call it that – to his way of thinking will be fully aired in court. I'm wondering though . . . would you be prepared to give evidence about your relationship with Richard?'

'Of course I would if it wouldn't do more harm than good.'

'I think perhaps you might be able to make the jury understand better than any words of mine could do exactly how you felt about each other.' He paused a moment, regarding her rather earnestly. 'Tell me something, Miss Norton. Did you get yourself up deliberately as the girl next door before you came to see me?'

She gave a gasp, and for a moment he thought she was going to burst into angry denial. Then, seeing the rather droll look he gave her, she suddenly began to laugh. 'How did you guess?' she asked. 'But as a matter of fact it wasn't for you, Mr Maitland, it was because I wanted to see Jamie, and I thought perhaps if I looked just a little bit dowdy his aunt might be more willing to let us have some time together.'

'I see.' The look of amusement was very marked now. 'I shall talk to Mr Conway and see what he thinks about calling you as a witness. If we do decide to do so your present rig would be very suitable, but don't be tempted to overdo it.'

'I won't,' she said rather doubtfully.

'And you no longer think I'm likely to get up in court and denounce you as the scarlet woman?'

'You're laughing at me, Mr Maitland. I never thought that, I was only afraid that the jury —'

'We'll do our best between us to scotch that. But make no mistake about it, if you appear as a witness you'll be giving Counsel for the Prosecution a chance to have a crack at you, and there's no telling what he may ask you.'

'If you think it will help I can put up with that.'

'Good girl,' he told her approvingly. 'Now, you said you wanted to talk about Jamie too. Have you seen him?'

'No, that's why . . . I came here yesterday, Mr Maitland, I very rarely miss a show so the director was really very understanding even though it meant missing the Saturday night performance. And then I went round in the late afternoon to the address Richard had given me, only I didn't manage to see his son.'

'Why did you want to do so?'

'Richard had told me he'd explained me to him after the first quarrels he had with Laura. I wanted to make Jamie understand two things. The first was that there was no way on earth his father could ever have done such a thing, and the other was that if things turned out well and we were able to marry I'd be very, very happy to have him with us. Children can get such strange ideas into their heads.'

'Jamie's twelve.' No need to mention his own talk with the boy.

113

'Yes, and I'm not at all sure that isn't the worst age of all. Perhaps I was foolish, but it seemed important to try to make him understand those things myself, because I can't imagine anything worse than for him to think that his father quite callously plotted to have his mother killed.'

'Were you able to convince him?'

'I never saw him. At least . . . I'd better tell you exactly what happened. A nice looking woman came to the door, and her greeting was a bit cool but I thought perhaps she took me for someone from one of the newspapers or something like that. She said she was Laura's sister, Amanda, and when I told her who I was her manner got cooler than ever if that was possible. I don't blame her, you know, but I asked her if I could come in for a moment to explain what I wanted, and after a little hesitation she pulled the door open. She took me into a sitting room and I tried to tell her what I've told you, and she was quite polite, even sympathetic, so that I realised my arriving on the doorstep unannounced like that must have been rather a shock to her. But she said there was no question of Jamie needing any protection besides what his mother's family could give him, and when I asked if I could talk to him at least, she thought about it for a while but then said she was sure it would only upset him more than ever.'

'I think she was wrong.'

'Do you? I couldn't argue with her . . . I mean, I couldn't be sure. So after we'd talked for a little longer I came away. And that was when I got a glimpse of Jamie, at least I'm sure it was Jamie because he's so like Richard. He pulled open a door at the back of the hall and looked out, and Amanda told him rather sharply to go back to his book. But then she said to me when the door was closed again that she'd make it up to him as soon as I'd gone, only the whole thing had been such a shock to him that she was terrified of making it worse. And of course I could understand that, not just knowing that Richard had been arrested, but losing his mother like that too.'

'You'd like Jamie,' said Maitland seriously. 'He came to see me yesterday, just as you have done. And . . . I still don't know if I did the right thing, but I'm sure I left him with the impression that I was quite convinced of his father's innocence. Because whatever happens I agree with you . . . I don't think it can do him any good to have doubts on that score.'

'You're telling me you don't believe in Richard yourself, Mr Maitland,' she said quietly but almost accusingly.

'I want to believe in him,' said Antony, which was as near to the truth as he could come at the moment. 'And perhaps you can understand that that makes me doubt my own judgement all the more. After all,' he defended himself, 'I've only met him once and that not in the best of circumstances.'

'No, I understand. And you don't want to persuade me as you say you persuaded Jamie –'

'I'm paying you the compliment of trying to be honest with you, Miss Norton. If you'd seen Jamie he'd have told you I promised him to do what I could for his father, even before we get into court. Unfortunately, that's not very much. I've asked Mr Willard this, of course, and he tells me he can think of nobody who might have wanted his wife dead. But he's under circumstances of great strain, and perhaps not thinking very clearly. Has he ever mentioned anything to you that might give you some idea –?'

'Nothing, nothing at all.'

'Well, it has occurred to me that the grudge must equally have been against him. The evidence is such that if he's innocent –'

'If,' said Mary sadly.

'I'm afraid at this stage I must put it that way. If he's innocent it means that somebody is deliberately trying to prove otherwise. Do you know of anybody with so serious a grudge against him?'

She shook her head, but she thought for a moment before she replied. 'Small jealousies, small disagreements, those aren't the kind of things you're thinking of, are they?'

'Not unless the person concerned is definitely unbalanced. But the more I think of it the more I feel that must be the case. To go to such lengths . . . and yet I know from my own experience that it's quite possible. The human mind seems to have an infinite capacity for self-deception.'

Afterwards he wondered whether Mary had been listening to him. 'I think,' she said, 'that if it were someone with a hate against Richard it would have to be someone he was getting in the way of professionally. And in the repertory circuit that doesn't really arise. Momentary irritation, yes of course. Richard has had an established position for a number of years with the Rothershaw Players as their leading man. That wouldn't worry his older colleagues, who play character parts, and if a promising youngster comes along there are any number of other companies for him to try his luck with. I suppose I can't give an absolute guarantee that someone he's encountered recently may not be unbalanced in the way you think, but if they are I certainly can't put a name to them.'

'I can't say I thought it was a very good line to follow anyway. Though there's nothing to stop its being a grudge of very long standing. Mr Conway has your address, hasn't he, if we want to get in touch with you?'

'Yes, of course he has.'

'What are you going to do now?'

'Go back to Rothershaw, I suppose,' she said rather drearily. 'Mr Conway – I always think of him as Chris because that's how Richard spoke of him – told me it wouldn't be advisable for me to try to go to the prison.'

'I think he's right about that. I'm supposed to be lunching with the Conways but I can easily put them off if you'll give me the pleasure of lunching with me before you go.'

'No, I don't think I feel like eating anything, and I have my car so I can leave at any time.'

'Some coffee at least,' he suggested. Mary refused that too, and a few minutes later he found himself alone again.

II

By the time Maitland arrived at Ingleton Crescent, which was an easy walk from the hotel though rather a chilly one, he found that Tony, though he had come nowhere near to solving his puzzle yet, had got over his initial preoccupation with it sufficiently to wish to regale them with a detailed description of all the steps he had taken so far towards its unravelling. Since he had been so quiet the evening before it seemed only fair to listen, and it wasn't until Chris got out the car and they were on their way to Dr Hargreaves's home that Antony had a chance to tell him about Mary Norton's visit. 'I can't make up my mind myself whether it would be a good idea to call her or not,' he concluded,' so it's up to you to make up your mind about that. I'll go along with anything you suggest.'

'I'll think about it,' said Chris noncommittally. For a moment he was engaged, in his cautious way, in achieving a left turn into a street of prosperous-looking detached houses. 'Dr and Mrs Hargreaves live at the far end,' he said. 'Do you still think you're right that they'd be glad of the money that Jamie would bring with him?'

'People are always in need of money, it's the first rule in the book as Jenny would say,' Antony told him. 'Seriously though, I've heard of districts where everyone knew the mortgages were so high that the owners couldn't get credit at any of the stores and had to subsist almost exclusively on a diet of sausage and mash.'

Chris grinned at that, but not as though he was really amused. He had been rather quiet throughout luncheon, and Antony had the feeling that he was just beginning to take in the difficulties that lay ahead of them, as he had realised them himself from the beginning; though of course at that time he hadn't had the same personal interest in the affair, except insofar as it affected Chris and Star. But now it was different, the familiar feeling of responsibility was back.

117

There were Richard and Mary, both of whom he was inclined to like, and and above all there was Jamie, who was relying on him for some sort of a miracle. If Richard Willard was indeed guilty there was nothing he could do to save the other two from suffering along with him, but he was beginning to doubt increasingly whether the answer was quite as simple as that. In any case he couldn't risk it, couldn't condemn the man in his own mind till all the evidence was in. And more and more his talk with Grandma Duckett was repeating itself endlessly in his thoughts. Something that had been said . . . something that had not been said . . . he couldn't make up his mind about it, but he had a growing conviction that the answer to his problem was to be found in the talk they had had together. He'd have to see her again, but what was the use of that unless he could somehow convince her of Richard Willard's innocence . . . otherwise she'd never volunteer information that might be damaging to another person.

Chris's words broke into his thoughts. 'Here we are, Antony, aren't you going to get out?' It was indeed a handsome place, right at the end of the road with fields beyond it. Perhaps that was why Laura had insisted on remaining in the house Richard had bought for her, keeping up with her brother rather than with the Joneses. 'Unless Dr Hargreaves has been called out,' Chris added encouragingly, 'we'll have plenty of time for our talk with them and to get you back to your train.'

'Yes, I'm sorry, I was thinking,' Antony apologised. He levered himself out of the car, and waited for Chris to come round to join him. 'Amanda Hargreaves didn't seem to bear me any malice for being involved in Willard's defence,' he said as they walked up the drive. 'I wonder how the good doctor will feel about it.'

'He sounded quite civilised on the phone,' Chris reassured him.

'That's good. Anyway, who lives may learn,' said Maitland absently. He was looking about him as he went, taking in the well-cared-for look of both house and grounds. That could be deceiving as he knew well enough, but most likely Chris was in the right of it and there was no lack of money.

In the meantime Conway had rung the bell, and a moment later the door was opened to them by a tall, thin man who stood back saying, 'Come in, come in,' in quite a welcoming way. 'I'm Henry Hargreaves,' he went on. 'You must be Dr Conway's son,' he added, looking at Chris. 'You're very like your father. And this, I suppose, is Mr Maitland.' Later as they talked together Antony was to recognise in him a distinct likeness to his sister Amanda, but in those first moments it only struck him that they were physically very unlike each other.

He left it to Chris to make the proper responses, the condolences, the apologies for troubling the Hargreaves at such a time. 'We all have our jobs to do,' said Henry, leading the way towards the drawing room. 'Isn't that so, Maria?' he added in a hopeful tone as they went in.

It was a comfortable room, though perhaps a little too tidy for Maitland's taste. The woman who was seated by the fire was also comfortable-looking, not very tall, round-faced, a little overweight, and with dark hair that showed signs of premature greying. But the illusion was spoiled when she turned her head and gave the two newcomers a decidedly inimical stare. 'Mr Conway and Mr Maitland,' said Dr Hargreaves rather hurriedly. 'My wife, gentlemen.'

Mrs Hargreaves didn't give Chris time to go into his spiel again. 'So I suppose,' she said rather coldly. 'And since my husband has agreed to see you, you'd better come in and sit down. Though why you should expect our help in protecting dear Laura's murderer I cannot think.'

Chris advanced warily but with Antony, who perversely was beginning to enjoy himself, close at his heels. 'Until the trial is over –' he began, but she didn't allow him to finish.

'Yes, I know all about that, Mr Conway.' Like her husband she was in doubt about which of them was which.

119

'But if you can tell me who else could have had a motive –' She didn't even try to complete the sentence.

Chris gave one agonised look in his friend's direction. Antony came forward and took a chair next to Mrs Hargreaves, pulling it forward slightly so that he could look at her directly. 'Don't you see, that's exactly why we're here? You and Dr Hargreaves of all people must know something of Mrs Willard's friends. And enemies,' he added, seeing her doubtful look.

'My wife is very naturally upset,' Henry Hargreaves put in from the chair he had taken at the other side of the hearth. 'I think I can assure you that my sister had no enemies. She lived very quietly, she was a gentle person and I'm sure that she never gave offence to anybody. Certainly not the kind of offence that would lead to a dreadful thing like this.'

'Motives for murder are as diverse as the people who commit them,' said Antony. 'What you might feel was a quite inadequate reason –'

'I consider any reason at all to be inadequate, Mr Maitland.'

'Yes, I'm sure you do. I'm only trying to say that . . . well, that the slightest thing may trigger some people off.' Again as he spoke there was that stirring in his mind of some idea that he couldn't quite grasp. 'I'm sure, Dr Hargreaves, that neither you nor Mrs Hargreaves would wish there to be a miscarriage of justice.'

'Certainly not. Are you trying to tell us that you believe Richard to be innocent?'

'He'll be pleading Not Guilty.'

'But that's just a form' said Maria Hargreaves, rather surlily. 'I won't have it!'

'I don't quite understand you, madam.'

'You'll try to get Richard off, and if you succeed he'll marry that woman and Jamie will go to live with them. I wouldn't like to have that on my conscience, Mr Maitland, that's what I mean.'

'I have a great regard for Jamie.'

'Have you seen him?'

'He came to see me at the hotel.'

'That's Amanda all over.' This time her glare was for her husband. 'Jamie should be here with us, then nothing like that could have happened.'

'It was his own idea.'

'Well, if you think a child his age should be free to roam about the town at will, Mr Maitland, I can assure you I don't agree with you. But it's absolutely ridiculous that Amanda, with no experience with young people whatever, should have the care of him even for a short time. As soon as the trial's over I can assure you we shall be taking steps to see that he comes to us.' Her expression softened as she thought of her nephew. 'He's a dear boy, and I know we can make it up to him.'

'Do you really think, Mrs Hargreaves, that even the most loving home – which I'm sure you'd give him – could make up for the loss of both his parents?'

'You're speaking of something over which we have no control,' Dr Hargreaves put in. 'Jamie, poor lad, is in a very unfortunate position, and I agree with my wife that we are the best people to try to put that right. As you point out I don't suppose we shall quite succeed but we'll do our best.'

'I don't see why we shouldn't succeed,' said Maria Hargreaves. 'Laura lived so quietly I'm sure the poor boy must have been lonely sometimes. That won't happen when I have the care of him, I can assure you of that.'

'I'm sure you're right, Mrs Hargreaves, but we're getting away from the question of Mrs Willard's friends.'

'A friend wouldn't have killed her.'

'No, but someone she believed to be her friend might have had some real or imagined cause of grievance against her.'

'You're talking of someone deranged, I think,' the doctor put in. 'As we both told you, Laura lived very quietly. After Richard left her I know she felt hurt that some of the couples they had been friendly with didn't include her in their activities any more. Perhaps that gave her a distrust of people, certainly I wouldn't say she had any really intimate friends.'

'She was engaged to be married.'

'That's rather different,' said Henry with a slight smile.

'I suppose it is. Before I go on, can we clarify one point? When Mr and Mrs Willard separated, whose idea was it in the first place?'

'I believe it was Laura who gave their marriage the *coup de grâce*, but I always held Richard to blame for having neglected her.'

'You don't think then that as soon as Jamie was old enough it might not have been a good idea for her to accompany her husband when his work took him away from home?'

'A child should have a feeling of security,' said Maria positively.

Is a broken home security? Maitland thought, but he didn't speak the words aloud. Instead, 'You mentioned Mrs Willard's intention of getting a divorce from her husband in order to re-marry,' he said. It was only later that he realised that wasn't completely accurate, but in any case the statement served its purpose and nobody contradicted him. 'Had you met Mr Eardley?'

'Naturally we had.'

'And what do you think of him?'

'You're not trying to insinuate, Mr Maitland, that he might have had some kind of motive?' said Dr Hargreaves.

'I'm not insinuating anything. I'm trying to get a picture of Mrs Willard's life ... I'm sure you've heard that a knowledge of the victim is of the first importance in a case like this.'

'Yes, I suppose you're right about that.' Henry Hargreaves sounded a little mollified, though a moment ago his tone had been sharp. 'I can't say I took to the man, his ideas were a little too puritanical for my liking, but if he made Laura happy I'd have forgiven him anything.'

'Yes, I see. How did you feel about him, Mrs Hargreaves?'

'He had rather strict ideas, as Henry says, but I don't think he'd have interfered with Jamie visiting us. In fact he said to me that Laura had been leading altogether too solitary a life, he meant to take her abroad when his holidays came round, and for short trips on long weekends. Jamie could have come to us so that they'd have their holidays alone together.'

'I see.' He smiled at her, and for the first time got a glimmer of a smile in return. 'So you'd at least have had no objection to the marriage.'

'It wasn't my place to object, but I do think there's nothing worse than loneliness,' she assured him earnestly.

'I'm quite sure you're right.' He hesitated a moment and then took the plunge. 'Are you seeing Jamie at the moment?'

'Not so much as we'd like.'

'There's been a slight coolness between my wife and my sister Amanda,' Dr Hargreaves explained. 'We both felt the proper place for Jamie was with us, but Amanda had Richard's agreement to the present arrangement, and until things are a little more settled it doesn't seem right to interfere.'

'Well, when you do see him ... you'll think I'm interfering, but please don't take it that way.' He was addressing himself to Maria Hargreaves now. 'He came to me in great distress because he'd talked openly to his father about his dislike for Lionel Eardley. I think I managed to reassure him.'

'Do you mean you've told him you believe his father to be innocent?'

'I didn't tell him anything exactly, but he was only too willing to persuade himself. What I wanted to ask you was ... couldn't you leave his illusions intact? If they are illusions, of which I'm by no means sure.'

'I wouldn't do anything to hurt Jamie, Mr Maitland.'

'No, I'm sure you wouldn't.' He turned again to Dr Hargreaves. 'That seems to be that,' he said, 'and not much help to Mr Conway and me, I'm afraid. I suppose you've no other relations who might know a little more about Mrs Willard's friends?'

'There's only my mother, and, poor soul, she's quite beyond helping you, I'm afraid.'

'I'm sorry to hear that.'

'She has an inoperable cancer. I haven't, as a matter of fact, even told her about Laura's death, and she's too far gone to realise how long it is since she's seen her.'

'That must be a great worry to you both on top of everything else.'

'I'm afraid it's reached the stage where it will be a relief in a way to know that she's gone, which may happen at any moment. Not because we shan't miss her, we do that already, but because of her own pain and bewilderment. She's drugged most of the time, of course, but when she comes round . . . but you didn't come here to talk about our troubles.'

'No, and I'm very sorry, as Mr Conway said when we arrived, to have intruded on you at such a time. Even more sorry now that you've told me this. I hope you'll forgive us . . . both of you.'

It seemed they had. Maria Hargreaves said, 'Goodbye,' quite graciously, and Dr Hargreaves let them out in quite as friendly a way as he had admitted them.

'That's a compassionate man,' said Antony when they were in the car again.

'I thought you suspected him of having had his sister shot,' said Chris drily.

'People are such a mass of contradictions that the two things might well go together,' Antony assured him.

'As for compassion, I'd have said the same about Mrs Hargreaves.'

'Even after the way she scared you when we first went in,' asked Antony quizzically.

'She thawed quite a bit, and she's genuinely concerned for Jamie.'

'Yes, but there's a little self-interest mixed up in that. If

124

they arranged it I'd say that wanting a child is the motive, even more than the money.'

'If,' said Chris. 'I don't believe it for a moment. For one thing the method would never occur to a doctor, of all people, he'd have much more subtle methods at his disposal.'

'What *do* you think then? Had Laura some hidden life that nobody we've seen so far knew anything about?'

'I don't know, Antony. Did I bring you here on a wild goose chase?'

'Now, don't you start having doubts.'

'You have them yourself. Or have you changed your mind?'

'I don't know, Chris, there's something I can't put my finger on.' They were turning into Cargate again, a street which sometimes seemed to Antony to lead everywhere you wanted to go in Arkenshaw. He glanced at his watch. 'We shall just have time to get a cup of tea in the station buffet before it's time for my train,' he said.

'If you can call it tea,' Chris growled. But he too glanced at his watch, and seeing that there was obviously not time to call in at Ingleton Crescent made no further objection to the plan.

III

Antony arrived home in time for dinner and found, without surprise, that Sir Nicholas and Vera had forgone their usual Sunday evening concert and had invited themselves to join the party. Or to put it more accurately, that his uncle had done so; Vera, he suspected, would be quite capable of doing the same thing if it ever became necessary, though her methods would be somewhat less arbitrary.

Meg and Roger were also present, and as Maitland had had a drink on the train they were able to proceed to the table almost immediately on his arrival. Sir Nicholas was quite capable of inconsistency when the spirit moved him, but the rule he insisted on without any variation was that shop should be totally excluded at mealtimes. It was therefore not until later, when the table was cleared and they were all gathered together round the fire, that Antony was able to give a rather sketchy account of his activities in Arkenshaw. 'So you see, I might have spared myself the journey until later in the week,' he concluded. 'Chris was being optimistic when he thought there might be something I could do.'

'I see you don't mean to tell us your real thoughts as to your client's guilt or innocence,' said Sir Nicholas rather tartly.

'I haven't any,' Maitland protested. 'And I've a bone to pick with you, Meg. You never told me Willard was living with a woman not his wife. I don't think you even mentioned that they were separated.'

'Gossip, darling,' said Meg.

'That's all very well, but would it still have been gossip if Counsel for the Prosecution had got up and sprung it on me in court?'

'Well, you seem to know all about it without my intevention,' said Meg, 'so I don't see that it matters at all.'

But if Maitland had wished to create a diversion he had succeeded well enough. Sir Nicholas and Vera, speaking in chorus, took it upon themselves to explain to Meg the importance of knowing the worst, and somehow when the subject was exhausted (though Meg was probably still far from convinced) there were no further questions about his trip or the way he intended to deal with the case, except one rather caustic query from his uncle as to whether he was quite sure that nobody had tried to murder him while he was in the North. Antony replied in kind, but the stiff way he moved that evening had proclaimed his tiredness from the moment he arrived, and none of the visitors stayed very late. Jenny took one look at her husband and suggested an early night and they talked very little after that, except that he took the opportunity to congratulate her on not having started any major project during his absence. 'Which is just as well,' he added, 'seeing that I got back so quickly.'

Downstairs, however, Sir Nicholas and Vera were not yet ready to retire. 'Think I was wrong,' said Vera, accepting a small supplementary measure of brandy.

'How do you mean, my dear?' Sir Nicholas helped himself rather more liberally and seated himself opposite her. 'Though I rather think I know,' he added thoughtfully.

'Of course you do. Said Antony had been much more upset about that Briggs business than I'd realised, but he looks fagged to death tonight, and that usually means he's worried.'

Sir Nicholas was quite ready to accept a certain looseness of speech from his wife which he would have condemned roundly in his nephew. 'When you've known him as long as I have, Vera,' he said, 'you'll know that means he's almost certainly decided that his client's innocent, and can't think of any way of proving it. I'd also make a guess – for your ears only, my dear – that he's got a shrewd suspicion who the guilty party may be.'

'What is it that nice Superintendent Sykes always says? When you know where to look –'

'That's all very well so far as the police are concerned,' said Sir Nicholas, 'but Antony isn't in a position to pursue that kind of inquiry. And to get them to act would take a good deal of persuasion on his part, particularly as there's an extremely good circumstantial case against his client, and as one of their own men was killed as a direct consequence of Willard's alleged actions.'

'I can see that all right,' Vera agreed. 'Always said, though, it's a mistake to get too deeply involved with a client's affairs.'

'If I've told Antony that once I've told him a hundred times,' Sir Nicholas agreed. 'He said – you heard him of course – that he has a great respect for Star Conway's opinion, but I wouldn't mind betting it's his own that's weighing with him. There's also the boy to consider, Antony

127

doesn't want him to be virtually orphaned, and when he said that, I though I detected a certain fellow feeling.'

'Difficult to see how anyone but the husband could have wanted to murder the woman,' said Vera. 'Don't like the cold-blooded aspect of the affair,' she added.

'Well, we must hope that the night will bring counsel,' said Sir Nicholas, not very optimistically. 'Though if I were a betting man I would lay you odds, my dear, as I believe the expression is, that the first thing Antony will do tomorrow will be to get in touch with Sykes.'

'Police obviously know a good deal about Porson, but I don't see how that'll help.'

'I don't suppose it will, but it's part of trying everything, which I sometimes think is Antony's principal creed so far as his work is concerned. As for his tiredness, it's mainly that damnable shoulder of his and there's nothing to be done about that.'

'No. Pity.' Vera sipped her cognac. 'One thing, Nicholas, for once you won't mind him getting mixed up with the police if he does talk to Superintendent Sykes as you expect.'

'No, and that's a relief. But this time there's also the question of organised crime being involved. I don't want him mixing himself up with that side of the business.'

'Surely he's got more sense.'

'Sense is a word you must never use in connection with our nephew,' said Sir Nicholas. 'I'm sure you realise that by now, my dear. Of course, I may be all wrong about his intentions,' he added more hopefully, 'but I couldn't help feeling that he was a little over-eager to change the subject tonight.'

Monday, 3rd February

For years Maitland had been avoiding visiting Scotland Yard, except when circumstances constrained him to do so. Now, however, his long feud with Chief Superintendent Briggs a thing of the past, he went there quite cheerfully the following morning when a telephone call revealed the fact that his old friend Sykes was rather overwhelmed with work at the moment and would appreciate not having to come into the City, even with the temptation of a leisurely lunch thrown in.

Superintendent Sykes's office was a shade more glorious than the one he had been allotted as Chief Inspector, which wasn't, Maitland considered, saying very much. However, he looked round appreciatively and grinned at the detective. 'They're spoiling you, Superintendent,' he said.

'Now then, Mr Maitland,' said Sykes in automatic reproof. He was a square-built man who looked more like a farmer than the very astute police officer he was, though Antony always added to this description a rider to the effect that the farmer had done a good deal at market that day and therefore had some cause for self-satisfaction. Sykes's voice still held some traces of his north country upbringing, though when he reverted to dialect it was generally in moments of stress, or sometimes as a deliberate sign of friendliness intended to be reassuring. Over the years the two men had had many dealings together, sometimes as allies and sometimes as adversaries, the result of which had been that a firm friendship had grown up between them and that each regarded himself as in some way indebted to the other. Recent events had only served to cement their alliance.

Every conversation with Sykes had inevitably to be preceded by a careful inquiry as to the health and well-being of the members of the household at Kempenfeldt Square. Maitland naturally responded by asking about Mrs Sykes, and remarked, on being reassured that she was in good health, 'And reet chuffed about your promotion, I expect.'

Sykes chose to reply in kind. 'Aye, she is an all. For that matter, Mr Maitland, I'm a bit chuffed myself but as I told you –'

'You're pressed for time, I know.' The chair Antony had taken was rather less penetential than the ones reserved for clients in his own office. He wriggled now into a more comfortable position. 'Still, you've got to do something to deserve all this glory,' he remarked.

At this Sykes smiled sedately but did not reply. After a moment Maitland went on, 'You'll have guessed why I want to see you. This affair in Arkenshaw.'

'Yes, I guessed as much, and not only from your greeting. So far as I know it's the only murder on your list this term. Besides I heard from Fred Duckett you were taking a hand in the matter. He's not too pleased about that.'

'I'm sorry to learn of Inspector Duckett's displeasure, but a brief is a brief after all.'

'I didn't say he was displeased with you, Mr Maitland. You got him out of a pretty sticky situation once and he's grateful for it.'

'He's no need to be. I only did what any other counsel would have done.'

At that Sykes smiled again. 'It's this business of Jim Ryder being killed,' he said. 'Fred has a very high opinion of your ability and he doesn't want you getting the chap responsible found Not Guilty.'

'Well, he's angry with his daughter, and with his son-in-law, Chris Conway, for calling me in. But they really believe

130

in Richard Willard's innocence, you know.'

'The case against him is very strong,' said Sykes thoughtfully. He eyed his companion for a moment. 'Not strong enough to satisfy you, Mr Maitland?' he asked.

'It ought to be,' Antony admitted.

'Still you're not satisfied?' Sykes was insistent.

'Not entirely.'

'What do you know that the police don't?'

'Now don't start on that tack again,' Antony implored him. 'I don't know anything except the case for the prosecution, and the fact that Willard denies it. But – you must have had the same feeling yourself sometimes – there's something about it that doesn't smell quite right to me.'

'I don't need to ask you if you've realised the corollary if your client is innocent.'

'You mean that he's being framed. It can happen, as we both know very well.'

'Yes, Mr Maitland, but don't let your own experiences influence your judgement. I've warned you about that before.'

'That's occurred to me too, and I'm making a definite effort to be impartial. But there's also the fact that I like what I've seen of Willard, and I'm desperately sorry for his young son.'

'Have you seen the boy?'

'Yes, he came to me at the hotel. And I'll be frank with you, Superintendent –'

'Because you know it can't do any harm,' Sykes murmured.

'– what he told me only went to confirm that fact that his father had a very good motive indeed for wanting Mrs Willard dead. He was blaming himself –'

He broke off there, but Sykes wasn't slow to take his meaning. 'Poor lad,' he said. 'What did you say to him?'

'As far as I remember only that it wasn't for me to judge the matter. I admit he took it to mean I thought his father was innocent.'

'As you no doubt intended,' said Superintendent Sykes rather drily. 'However, it'd do the lad no good to be too disillusioned. Which brings me to the question, Mr Maitland – and I'm sorry if I seem to be rushing you – what exactly did you want to see me about?'

'There's nothing much I can do until we get into court and I can cross-examine the prosecution's witnesses. I've talked to Laura Willard's relations, but she seems to have led a very quiet life, and they couldn't give me a hint as to any possible enemies of hers.'

'There's something else I'm sure you've thought about, Mr Maitland. The Willards have been separated for a number of years, haven't they?'

'Seven years, so I understand.'

'And yet according to your theory –'

'It isn't exactly a theory yet.'

Sykes ignored that. 'According to your theory someone disliked them both enough to arrange to have Mrs Willard killed in a way that would incriminate her husband. I've heard a good deal about this from Fred Duckett – Constable Ryder's murder has made him take particular interest in the case, not unnaturally – and if this man Porson didn't go to The Bishop's Move to meet his principal and get instructions from him, as the prosecution will maintain, he can only have gone there with the deliberate intention of getting in touch with your client, and providing evidence against him. You'll also have seen the difficulty about that.'

'Porson's presence in Arkenshaw was only known by chance, and without that knowledge on the part of the police the case against Richard Willard would have been incomplete. I can't help feeling that Porson's principal must have had some plan to cover that, but as the hue-and-cry was raised almost immediately and the man's picture plastered all over the place it wasn't necessary to put it into operation.'

'There was still the matter of the witnesses to the meeting.'

'I know, and that would seem to bring us to the man Laura Willard wanted to marry, Lionel Eardley. He was the one who put the police onto the witnesses from The Bishop's Move, after their first inquiries there had revealed nothing. But I can't see why he should want Laura dead, let alone to incriminate Richard Willard. It couldn't have been a matter of self-protection merely. After all, whoever arranged this affair wouldn't know the London police had given the local chaps a line on Porson. If that hadn't happened Laura Willard would have been shot by an unknown gunman, Richard Willard would have had an alibi, and the affair would just have remained a mystery . . . except for Eardley's intervention.'

'So you think this man –?'

'I think that the fact that he went to the police with the information about the meeting at The Bishop's Move has some significance, but that's as much as I can say at the moment.' He broke off there and a rather startled look came into his eyes.

'You've thought of something, Mr Maitland,' said Sykes almost accusingly.

'I . . . no, it's too far-fetched. I was about to say, Superintendent, that the only approach I can make at the moment is through Porson, if I can possibly find out anything about the man. That's why I came to you.'

'And what do you intend to do with the information?'

'I don't know,' said Antony rather helplessly. 'But just at the moment the only line of defence I can see is to point out to the court that it's very unlikely that Richard Willard could ever have come into contact with him. The trouble is, of course, that seems to apply equally to anybody else I can think of with whom Laura Willard was acquainted.'

'Yes, I see your difficulty. You've considered the possibility, I suppose, that if you start inquiries from this end you may uncover the fact your client *did* have the opportunity of approaching Porson to do his dirty work for him.'

'Of course I've thought of that!' said Antony rather irritably.

'In any case there's very little I can tell you. We've known of his activities for the past ten years, or to be fair I should say suspected, because until this last case where we have Constable Ryder's dying statement there's never been anything like proof against him.'

'Is murder his only ocupation?'

'He and his associates have had, I should say, a hand in pretty well every kind of racket you can think of that might prove profitable to them, either directly or because they were hired for some specific job.'

'A sort of Universal Aunts in reverse,' said Antony.

'If you care to put it that way. But heaven help us if the ladies ever decide to engage in that sort of activity.'

'The female of the species is more deadly than the male?'

'Something like that.'

'Did Porson have a girlfriend?'

'He was and is married. I'm quite sure that Mrs Porson knows something at least of his activities, I don't see how she could have avoided doing so. But there's no proof there either, and as long as she plays the innocent –'

'You mentioned his associates.'

'Yes, Mr Maitland, and that's as far as I'm going to go.'

'Oh, come now, Superintendent –'

'No, Mr Maitland. I'm not having your murder on my conscience,' said Sykes flatly. 'That's what it would amount to; they don't like people asking questions.'

'But I thought Porson was their First Murderer.'

'Only when marksmanship was needed. The rest of them . . . well, they haven't a scruple among them and that's a fact.'

'You must have had them under observation. You knew when Porson left London, for instance.'

'Now, you know as well as I do, Mr Maitland, that with the manpower at our disposal we can't keep anything like round-the-clock surveillance on all the villains in London. It was pure chance that Porson was seen boarding that train, and we weren't sure where he was going – it might have been Leeds or Arkenshaw – but we warned the police at each place on principle. Of course, since the murders, there've been questions asked, and if you want the honest opinion we've come to it's that none of his friends have the faintest idea where he is. He seems to have vanished off the face of the earth.'

'And is Mrs Porson equally ignorant?'

'Yes, I think so. Of course her place is under observation, but he hasn't come home.'

'Let's see how it'll look from his point of view. He seems to have had no idea the Arkenshaw police were keeping tabs on him.'

'Which is a very good mark for them,' Sykes pointed out.

'It is indeed. Well, he shoots Laura Willard, and then he comes down from the roof of the Imperial Café and bumps smack into Constable Ryder. He shoots him because he's a witness, not because he knows who he is. But then later he's almost sure to have seen a newspaper somewhere and found out what he'd really done. That would have put a scare into him; he'd know every policeman in the country would be after his blood.'

'Constable Ryder's statement was never published in the newspapers.'

'No, but I think it would put the wind up him all the same. He must have guessed that he was being followed. A car was stolen and found abandoned in Leeds, with no tell-tale fingerprints, I imagine?'

'That's right. There's no actual proof that Porson was the thief, but he didn't get away by train and he didn't get away by air, so unless he got a lift, in which case I imagine the person who picked him up would have come forward by now –'

'Unless he's dead too. It's a dangerous business picking up hitch-hikers. But no' – he contradicted himself – 'whoever it was would have been reported missing by now, or if a body had been found the police would never have missed a clue like that.'

'You're quite right, they wouldn't. But the point doesn't

135

arise because there was no such clue.'

'Have the gang's operations been exclusively in London?'

'Porson's have, so far as we know. At least there's been no job done with his signature, if I can put it that way, in any other part of the country until Mrs Willard's death.'

'And the rest of the gang?'

'Oh, they get about a bit as you can imagine. But London's where the main action is.'

'Have any of them been caught?'

'A number of them are inside now. But I've got a feeling, Mr Maitland, that you're talking for the sake of it, hoping that I'll change my mind. And I tell you straight I won't do it.'

Antony knew the other man quite well enough to realise that he meant what he said. 'Couldn't you at least give me Mrs Porson's address?' he asked not very hopefully.

'No,' Sykes said flatly. 'I've told you she isn't the innocent she pretends to be, and to have you visit her would be just as good as giving your name and address to the rest of them.'

'Perhaps she's in the telephone book.'

'Yes, perhaps she is.' Sykes's patience was not altogether inexhaustible. 'I told you the house was under observation, Mr Maitland, and if I hear of you having been anywhere near it I'll slap a charge of obstructing the police on you so quickly you won't know what hit you.'

'Come now, Superintendent, you wouldn't do that to an old friend.'

Sykes couldn't help smiling at the injured innocence in his visitor's tone, but, 'It's for your own good,' he said in a scolding voice. 'You'll not help your client by being dead or at best in hospital when the case comes on.'

'No, I suppose you're right.' Sykes gave him a suspicious look, but evidently was satisfied with what he saw.

'Where do *you* think Porson is, Superintendent?' Antony asked.

'If I knew that, Mr Maitland, I'd have him under arrest.'

'Yes, so I suppose.' Antony sighed and got to his feet.

'Chris seems to think the case will come up about the end of this week,' he said. 'Perhaps you'll be less busy when I get back from Arkenshaw, and can come and have dinner with us. Jenny will never remember to give you your correct title, I'm sure of that, but I daresay you'll forgive her.'

'I'd like that, Mr Maitland.' Sykes was on his feet too. 'And try to keep out of trouble, lad,' he advised.

Antony turned with his hand on the door-knob. 'Trouble?' he asked. 'How can I get into trouble now that Chief Superintendent Briggs has retired?'

'You know well enough what I mean. There's more than one kind of trouble,' said Sykes. 'And if I know you,' he added, as the door closed gently behind his visitor, 'if there's anything like that going you'll be the one to find it.'

Tuesday, 4th February

Antony had given Jenny a blow-by-blow account of his
talk with Superintendent Sykes and he repeated this to
Sir Nicholas and Vera when they came to dinner the
next evening. 'I suppose I should say, thank heavens
for the Superintendent's good sense,' said Sir Nicholas
caustically. 'Can you assure me, as I trust you've
already assured Jenny, that you've no intention of
taking the matter further on these lines?'

'How can I, Uncle Nick? I've no means of finding out
in the time at my disposal who the rest of the gang are,
and as for Mrs Porson . . . the trouble is I can see
Sykes's point of view. They want to get their hands on
the man, and even so small a matter as a visit from me
might inhibit him from returning home if she managed
to get a message to him. Besides, the police have
already asked her if she's any knowledge of who
approached him in this matter and got a dusty answer,
so I really don't see what good I could do.'

Sir Nicholas raised his glass, admired its contents for
a moment, and then set it down again without tasting
them. 'This is positively unnerving,' he said. 'Are you
perfectly sure, Antony, that you're feeling quite well?'

Maitland, standing a little to one side of the fire with
one shoulder leaning against the high mantel, grinned
down at his uncle. 'Quite sure,' he said. 'And you
needn't worry, any of you. Going to see Sykes at all was
a counsel of despair, and as he won't help me . . . I

know him well enough to realise when he means what he says.'

'Yet,' said Sir Nicholas, 'you don't look exactly despairing.'

'Uncle Nick, you've told me often enough, you and Vera both, that it is a fool's game to get personally involved in a case. I'm doing my best to follow your precepts . . . that's all.'

'If I could believe that –'

'Have I ever lied to you, Uncle Nick?'

'There have been times, as I'm sure you will not deny, my dear boy, when you have not been altogether open with me.'

'Well, in this case . . . will it content you if I say I shall do nothing more in the matter until I get Chris's phone call summoning me back to Arkenshaw? And that won't be until the case is about to come on.'

'Think you can believe him, Nicholas,' said Vera gruffly.

'I'm obliged for the assurance, my dear. I should, however, very much like to know, Antony, why – if this is true – you're looking so positively light-hearted.'

'If you must know, sir, it's because I've made up my mind that my client has been telling me the truth.'

'I see,' said Sir Nicholas ominously. 'Am I to understand that you are proposing to clear the whole matter up in the course of the trial? By a brilliant cross-examination of this man Eardley, for instance?'

'Not – not exactly, sir.'

'You will forgive me if I say that I find that reply distinctly evasive.'

That of course had been Maitland's intention. 'Will you be any happier, Uncle Nick, if I admit that I think it'll help to talk to him, and as things stand the only chance I have of doing so is in court,' said Maitland with a great air of candour. And beyond that, and the reiterated statement that until he heard from Chris there wasn't anything else he could do in the matter, he refused to be drawn.

Two snatches of conversation after the Hardings had left for their own quarters may however be not altogether irrelevant. 'Will it last?' Vera asked her husband bluntly.

'I don't quite understand you, my dear.'

'Antony's . . . what you call his light-heartedness. As far as I could see it was quite genuine.'

'For the moment, I think it was. He's made up his mind, against all the evidence, and whether he's done so just because he wants the wretched man to be innocent, I can't tell you. What I do know is that before he's finished, some of his previous doubts will have returned. And even if he's right it's going to come home to him sooner or later how impossible it is to prove. And when that happens, Vera –'

'He'll be in the depths again,' Vera concluded for him.

'Precisely. And there's nothing we can do about it –'

'Except stand by and help Jenny pick up the pieces.'

'That, my dear, is a very good assessment of the situation. But I don't think, from all I've heard, that there's the faintest doubt that this man Willard was responsible both for his wife's death, and for that of the unfortunate Constable Ryder. The only mystery about the whole affair is where this man Porson has got to, and we must just be thankful that Antony has seen the wisdom of leaving that side of things to the police.'

Jenny, however, tackled the matter from another angle. 'You've got an idea, Antony,' she said as soon as he had come back from seeing their uncle and aunt safely on their way.

'That sounds like an accusation, love,' he answered lightly.

'Yes, but have you?'

'The glimmer of an idea, Jenny, and I don't know

how much it's worth.'

'Tell me,' she invited.

'Not yet, love.'

'Why? Is it dangerous?'

'My dearest love, I swear if it were I'd tell you. The only reason I won't is because . . . can you understand that it's so tenuous that if I put it into words I may realise its futility myself and not go ahead with it? And for better or worse I do owe Richard Willard the best I can do for him.'

Jenny was frowning over the thought. 'Yes, I think I can understand that,' she said. 'I suppose I must just possess my soul in patience. But I do wish,' she added with a sigh, 'that the police had been able to find that awful man Porson. It's not that I'm worried, you know,' she insisted. 'But —'

'Of course not, love,' Antony agreed. And then, 'Bear with me, Jenny. I'm really not going to do anything stupid.'

Thursday, 6th February

The call from Chris came earlier than he had expected, the following morning in fact, so that on the Wednesday evening he again caught the late train to Arkenshaw.

'It's a miracle, of course,' said Chris while they were waiting for their case to be called the following morning.

'You mean that old Gilmour got through his list so quickly?' Maitland asked him. He looked from his instructing solicitor to his junior, a man called John Bushey with whom he had worked before, who belied his name by being almost completely bald, though that fact was hidden, of course, by the wig he was wearing. He was a man whom Maitland had often suspected of being without emotions of any kind, win or lose, it was all one to him. But he would follow his leader however difficult the going, and was to be valued for that. 'I think on the whole I'm glad the matter's being dealt with so quickly,' Antony added. 'I was finding it difficult to settle to anything else, and as far as I'm concerned His Lordship can ask as many questions as he damn well pleases.'

'I'll remind you of that,' said Bushey, with rather a boisterous laugh. 'As far as I recall, you're not over-fond of your opposite number either.'

'Anderson?' William Anderson, Q.C., was leading for the prosecution. 'I've nothing particular against him except that I've a feeling that he doesn't care much for me. But we can none of us expect to be universally beloved.'

'He's always so sure he's right,' Chris grumbled, and

142

Bushey glanced at him quickly so that Maitland thought he'd have liked to have said, 'and isn't he in this case?' But true to form the other man made no open comment, and a few minutes later their patience was rewarded and the case was called.

As far as Maitland was concerned that first day was a wasted one: a wilderness of facts that he knew perfectly well already, and whose interpretation no questions of his were able to shake. A worrying one too, because one look informed him that Richard Willard wasn't taking kindly to confinement, and as his evidence couldn't possibly be reached before the weekend his counsel couldn't help wondering in what sort of a state he'd be when the time came for him to leave the dock and go into the witness box.

Anderson's opening address took them to lunchtime, and was predictable enough. After the recess there followed the police evidence concerning the surveillance that had been kept on Porson's movements – in view of the nature of the charge there could be no objection to that on the grounds of irrelevance – and the medical evidence concerning Laura Willard's death. Mr Justice Gilmour was as full of questions as usual, and seemed in some odd way to resent the fact that there were not more interruptions from the defence. 'But there was really nothing to be gained,' said Maitland rather defensively to the other members of his team when the court adjourned.

'Tomorrow –' Chris began.

'Yes . . . tomorrow,' said Antony rather heavily. All the confidence he had felt in his ability to deal with the situation seemed to have left him now.

'They'll be calling Eardley,' said Chris rather impatiently.

'So they will.'

John Bushey had bundled his papers together and was ready to depart. 'The evidence from the pub,' he said, 'is the only chance we've got of gaining any points as far as the witnesses are concerned. Though of course,' he added, perhaps by way of consolation, 'there'll be things you can 'bring out when you address the jury.'

'Yes, I –' He broke off to call goodbye after his junior's retreating back. 'I suppose you haven't got anything on the two men who saw Willard and Porson talking together, Chris? No connection between them and Eardley, for instance.'

'My impression is that he isn't the sort of chap that they'd have made a friend of. Too straight-laced. I told you they both say they knew Richard by sight quite well, though they deny having ever spoken to him. And he can't help us there, he often talked to people in the pub but he never knew anyone's name. So unless he recognises either of them in court –'

'I don't think it would make any difference. It was just a passing thought. Eardley's the one I'm really interested in, but I don't know, Chris, I don't know. The whole thing will require very delicate handling.'

Chris looked as if he would like to say, 'I told you so,' but realising his companion's depressed mood he nobly refrained. 'You're dining with us,' he said. 'Star's expecting you.'

'I ought –'

'The best thing you can do is forget all about the case until the morning,' said Chris emphatically. 'It's like taking an exam, all the cramming in the world won't get you through if you leave it to the last moment.'

Maitland smiled at that. 'I suppose I should be grateful to you for only insinuating that I haven't read my brief,' he said. 'All right, Chris, I'll follow your advice, and send my apologies to the Bar Mess. Naturally I want to see Star and Tony.'

Afterwards he wondered whether Star had been rehearsing all day to find topics of conversation that might prove a distraction. It was noticeable, too, that Tony was allowed to stay up much beyond his usual bedtime. All in all the evening was a pleasant one, and it was a little later than he intended when he got back to the hotel. He called Jenny and hoped he had done a good job of hiding his feelings from her. It was true enough that the day had contained nothing that was unexpected. 'Will you be coming home for the weekend, Antony?' she asked.

'I still don't know, love. It will depend on what happens tomorrow.'

'All right then, I'll wait to hear from you.' They talked for a little longer, but sleep was still very far away for Antony when at last they said goodnight.

He made his preparations for bed, but then he hesitated. Chris's advice had been good, he knew that from experience, but perhaps after all there might be some advantage in looking at his brief again, at least as far as Lionel Eardley's evidence was concerned. The temptation was too great. He carried his briefcase over to the table by the window, and began to rummage through its contents. It was three in the morning before he gave up, but he had to admit that his researches hadn't left him any the wiser.

Friday, 7th February

I

The next morning's hearing began with a harrowing account of Constable James Ryder's dying statement. The picture was clearer now; he had been following Porson, and had seen him go into the lane behind the Imperial Café, where he had lost sight of him. A short time afterwards he had heard the shot, and a moment later footsteps clattering down the fire-escape. Porson couldn't have known he was being followed, and the lane was a dead end so that he must have felt it was unlikely that anyone would be about. Ryder had attempted to grapple with the fugitive, and there was no doubt in his mind that it was Porson who had shot him. Getting into the realms of speculation Superintendent Morrison, of the local CID, surmised that Ryder, realising that the shot must have been fired into the square, had known there would be plenty of people about to aid the victim if that were possible, and so had felt it his first duty to stop the assassin. Maitland didn't feel inclined to argue about that. The result had been tragic enough, without his trying to throw doubt on the wisdom of the constable's decision. He merely shook his head when Anderson glanced at him inquiringly, and Morrison was allowed to step down.

The prosecution had chosen to call the witnesses from The Bishop's Move before taking Lionel Eardley's evidence. The reason for that was obvious enough, opportunity first and then motive, which in this instance was the most telling part of their case. The landlord had recognised a photograph of Porson as a man who had come into the bar at opening time

146

several Sundays in succession during the previous December. On each occasion he had ordered one double scotch, and retired with it to a table in the corner. He had never noticed anyone speaking to him, but he was busy about his duties and might easily not have done so.

Maitland had just two questions, first pointing out that one man with a scar might very easily be mistaken for another with a similar disfigurement (and what was the use of that when various members of the police force had already testified that they had followed Porson to The Bishop's Move) and then asking whether the landlord also recognised the accused. Yes, of course, he liked the theatre himself so he'd always taken an interest in this particular customer, him being an actor there and all. Mr Willard had been a regular visitor for years, though so far as he could remember he hadn't been in much since the beginning of December. No, the witness had never seen him talking to the man with the scar. Which was all very well, but any favourable effect was completely demolished when Anderson chose to re-examine, and stressed the fact that lunchtime on a Sunday was always a busy time at The Bishop's Move.

There followed the two men who had witnessed the conversation between Richard Willard and the man with the scar. Their evidence differed only in a very slight degree, one of them saying that Richard Willard had taken his drink deliberately to the table where Porson was sitting, the other saying that he had thought at the time how earnestly the two men were conferring together. Neither was to be shaken in the identification of the photograph of Porson that had been introduced into evidence by the prosecution, and both, as Chris had said, knew Willard quite well by sight. Maitland did what he could, but neither of them was to be shaken in his story, his only small gain being the admission that the subject of the conversation had not been overheard.

The court had adjourned for the luncheon recess before the second of these men was called, and it was getting towards three o'clock when Lionel Eardley stepped into the witness box. While he was being sworn in and Anderson was taking him smoothly through the preliminary questions Maitland took the opportunity of studying him. A man of medium height with some pretensions to good looks, if you discounted the sharpness of his features which gave him a rather predatory look. He was neatly, almost foppishly dressed; a suit that had obviously not come off the peg, and some care had clearly been taken so that his tie, and his shirt, and the faint check in the material all blended harmoniously together. Perhaps, thought Antony, a little wryly, pride was not one of the sins that the Levellers recognised. Or perhaps they would call it proper pride or self-respect and as such find it easily forgiveable. But his impressions must wait, Anderson was getting down to his direct examination.

'First, I must ask you, Mr Eardley, whether you knew the deceased lady, Mrs Laura Willard?'

'I knew her very well.' His voice was a little high-pitched, but not unpleasantly so.

'Could you pehaps tell us something of your relationship with her?'

'Certainly. We were going to be married.'

'That would have had to have waited until her divorce went through, would it not?'

'Yes, but there was no difficulty about that. Her husband . . . the prisoner,' he added, glancing rather venomously at Richard, 'had left her seven years ago. And besides he was living with another woman.'

'My lord!' Maitland was on his feet. 'My friend has laid no groundwork for this accusation.'

'Mr Anderson?' said the judge, glancing up from his notes.

'I had not intended to ask this witness about that aspect of the matter, my lord. But evidence will be forthcoming that confirms his statement.'

'I see.' Mr Justice Gilmour turned to the witness. 'I wonder, Mr Eardley, how you came by that piece of information?'

'Common knowledge, my lord.'

148

'Here in Arkenshaw?'

'Among the company of players to which the prisoner belonged in Rothershaw. I suspected something of the sort, knowing what members of that profession are like, so I made my own inquiries. Well, I think I had a right to do so, considering the way things were between Laura and me.'

'Have you any further objection, Mr Maitland?'

'No, my lord. As the witness has been allowed to give vent to his spite against my client –'

'You will have the opportunity of addressing the jury later, Mr Maitland,' said Gilmour coldly. 'In the meantime you may proceed, Mr Anderson.'

'I am obliged to your lordship. Leaving aside the question of divorce, Mr Eardley, when did you ask Mrs Willard to marry you?'

'During the last week in November of last year.'

'Did she agree?'

'Oh yes, indeed.' That was said with a self-satisfied smirk, which Maitland, reprehensibly, would have given a good deal to wipe from the witness's face.

'Did you on that occasion have some discussion about the future?'

'Yes, we did. There were a number of matters to be settled, even though the wedding must be delayed by the unsavoury matter of the divorce.'

'Perhaps you can specify those matters a little more exactly, Mr Eardley?'

'There was the question of where we should live. But that was easily settled; Laura loved her home and I wouldn't have dreamed of depriving her of it. Then there was the question of religion.'

'Did you run into any difficulty there?'

'None at all. I am myself a member of the Levellers, we're not strong numerically but growing in influence, I believe. Laura had always been a chapel-goer, and quite readily agreed to accompany me to our services in future. In fact, I think I may say that what I was able to tell her about our beliefs impressed her very much.'

'So on these matters you were in complete harmony?'

'That is so.'

'But there was one difficulty that you foresaw?'

'Not exactly a difficulty, at least so far as Laura and I were concerned. It was the matter of her son, Jamie, and frankly I was worried about the boy.'

'Will you explain that to us please, Mr Eardley?'

'Heredity, sir, heredity. There's bad blood in the boy.'

Maitland was on his feet again. 'Does my learned friend intend to call expert witnesses on this point?' he asked in rather a too dulcet a tone.

'I'm sorry, my lord,' said Anderson rather quickly. 'The witness is giving his own opinion, which naturally isn't evidence, though you may feel it will explain the stand he took, and the events that followed.'

'The jury will disregard the remark,' said Gilmour automatically. 'Perhaps you should try, Mr Anderson, to prevent any further outbursts of this kind from your witness.'

'I shall certainly endeavour to do as your lordship wishes.'

'Then you may proceed.'

'Mr Eardley, without touching on any matter which may be contentious, will you tell us what your and Mrs Willard's intentions were concerning her son?'

'I thought she should be more strict with him,' said Eardley a little more cautiously now.

'And what besides?'

'I was worried about his father's influence over the boy. Laura was too soft-hearted, she had given her husband unrestricted access, which meant that he saw Jamie almost every week. I pointed out the dangers to her, and said that this practice must stop.'

'And did Mrs Willard agree?'

'Yes, she said she realised now that she had been careless. She would see Willard on the following Sunday when he came, and tell him she wanted a divorce, and that she could not allow him to see Jamie so often in future.'

'Did she tell you whether this conversation in fact took place?'

'Yes, it upset her very much. She said her husband had stormed at her and said he wouldn't take the matter lying down. I tried to comfort her with the reflection that when it came to the divorce the court was bound to be on our side. I'm glad to say that she saw the matter completely from my point of view and though she was upset by the unpleasantness that the prisoner's attitude would have led to, she was quite adamant that there would be no question of his seeing Jamie so frequently from then on.'

'And was that the end of the matter?'

'No, indeed. She had meant to refuse Jamie permission to go with his father that day, it was the first Sunday in December. But the boy slipped out, and the following week he was not to be found when Laura was ready to go with me to the Sunday service. Apparently he had gone to meet his father. There were angry words again when Willard brought the boy home, and the following week he came again, but that time also I was waiting for him with Laura.'

'Can you describe his attitude to us, Mr Eardley?'

'One of bitter anger. He said that Jamie had begged to be allowed to live with him and his paramour –'

'My lord. The witness is giving a deliberately false impression of the situation. When the divorce had gone through Mrs Willard had intended to marry again. Why should the same privilege not have been accorded to my client?'

'It is a matter of interpretation only, my lord,' said Anderson. 'At the time of which we are speaking –'

'Very well, Mr Anderson, very well. The jury will have taken your point, Mr Maitland, and I think that is all that should concern you.'

'If your lordship pleases.' Antony sat down again with an angry swirl of his gown. He was disliking the witness more and more every moment, and the account that Eardley was now giving, with some relish, of the quarrel that had

151

followed did nothing to diminish his distaste.

There was a good deal of repetition of what Anderson considered the most important points. Certainly by the time he had finished no one in the courtroom could have been in any doubt that Richard Willard was willing to fight, to go to any lengths as the witness had put it, so as not to have to relinquish some control over his son and his son's education, and above all not to have to forego his frequent companionship. But at last Counsel for the Prosecution had finished and handed his witness over to the defence.

Maitland got to his feet slowly, and stood for a moment contemplating the man who was giving evidence. Lionel Eardley was full of self-confidence (just the state of mind he would least have wished) but there was also a certain air of enjoyment about him which was probably what prompted counsel's first question.

'I suppose I should begin, Mr Eardley, by commiserating with you on your sad loss.'

To the witness at least the shaft went home. Maitland could only hope its effect was equally obvious to the jury. There was an almost dead silence before Eardley said, recovering himself, 'Thank you, sir. Laura's death was a great blow to me, though it isn't in my nature to make a great display of my grief. Besides' – he was getting into his stride now – 'what is grief for the loss of a loved one but selfishness? She, I am sure, has gone to a better place.'

'I think in this instance any of us would be willing to concede you a little selfishness, Mr Eardley, without blaming you too strongly. I'm glad at least to know that the pleasure you take in displaying your malice towards my client is not your only emotion.'

'My lord!' said Anderson, rising quickly. 'These insinuations against the witness –'

'I submit, my lord, that I am insinuating nothing that Mr Eardley has not already confirmed in his testimony. You don't like actors, do you, Mr Eardley?' he asked, turning back to the witness before the judge had time to reply.

152

'I think the depravity of the profession is only too well known,' said the witness. Maitland, watching the judge's reaction out of the corner of his eye, saw Gilmour shrug slightly, and pick up his pen again.

'Thank you for being so frank with me, Mr Eardley. That explains a good deal, as I am sure the members of the jury will agree.' He hoped he was right about that, not having very much respect for the collective intelligence of any body of twelve men and women chosen almost at random. 'Perhaps this attitude of yours may explain one slight inaccuracy in your testimony.'

'I've told nothing but the truth.'

'Have you indeed? You took the oath on the Bible, but I was beginning to wonder whether members of your particular sect . . . you'll forgive me, I know, if I am wrong, but I know so little about them.'

'We respect the Bible as a source of all truth. Literal truth,' he amplified.

'Then, I'm sure you won't mind my putting you right on this small point I mentioned, on which you must be . . . mistaken,' said Maitland. 'You said that my client left his wife, Mrs Laura Willard, seven years ago.'

'Yes, I did, and I was right.' He was definitely truculent now.

'The truth is rather, as I understand it, that the parties separated by mutual agreement, but that Mrs Willard was the one who requested her husband to leave.'

'I don't see that that makes any difference. He was the one that went away.'

'I'm afraid in the circumstances – the very serious circumstances, Mr Eardley – the court must demand absolute accuracy. Now about these quarrels you have cited between my client and the deceased. On consideration, wouldn't you perhaps admit that the intention to deprive a man of his son's company was a little hard?'

'I wasn't going to have any stepson of mine being subjected to such a bad influence.'

'How can you be sure Mr Willard was a bad influence on his son?'

'He's an actor, isn't he? Besides he was living in open sin.'

'How did you know that?'

'My lord!' said Anderson. 'My learned friend objected to this line of questioning from me.'

'I did, my lord,' said Maitland quickly. 'But my friend was able to convince me that I had been wrong in doing so.'

Gilmour smiled rather grimly. 'In that case, Mr Maitland, I see no reason why you shouldn't proceed.'

'Perhaps you'll be kind enough to answer my question, Mr Eardley. I asked you how you knew anything of my client's way of life.'

'Because I went to Rothershaw and asked some members of the repertory company there. One of them told me –'

'And you were willing to take an actor's word? Or that of an actress, as the case may be?'

'It wasn't only that,' said Eardley with a distinct note of triumph in his voice. 'I asked their landlady too. Willard and the woman's.'

'You own relationship with Mrs Willard, of course –'

'Was perfectly innocent,' the witness snapped.

'In one sense, yes, I'm sure it was. She was however, a married woman.'

'Separated,' said Eardley.

'I'm grateful to you for the correction.' (Chris, sitting behind him, thought, he's getting more like Sir Nicholas every minute.) 'There is another matter I must take up with you,' Maitland was continuing, 'which inexplicably my learned friend failed to touch on. It is the matter of the evidence from the public house, The Bishop's Move.'

'My lord!' said Anderson again. (He must be getting tired of these physical jerks, thought Antony irreverently.)

'Yes, Mr Anderson?'

'I –'

'I think what my friend wishes to say,' said Maitland kindly, when his learned opponent paused for a moment, 'is that it is quite irrelevant how the evidence from The Bishop's Move came to light.'

'Is that correct, Mr Anderson?'

'Certainly it is, my lord,' said Counsel for the Prosecution with an unfriendly look at his adversary. 'It is quite immaterial –'

'I submit, my lord, that my learned friend is over-simplifying the matter. I should hesitate to suggest that there had been a deliberate attempt to cover up what I must call a certain lack of assiduity on the police's part, but I also maintain that I have every right to go into the matter.'

Gilmour gave him a long hard stare. 'Very well, Mr Maitland, we'll see where this line of questioning takes us,' he said.

'I am obliged to your lordship. Now, Mr Eardley, perhaps you'll tell us, in your own words, something of your feelings during the weeks that followed Mrs Willard's death, and what you did in consequence of them.'

'Well, I was upset naturally –'

'Naturally,' agreed counsel smoothly.

'– but I wasn't in any doubt about who'd done it. I mean, it was obvious, wasn't it?'

'Let us be exact about this, Mr Eardley. When you say it was obvious who had done it, you mean more precisely who had arranged for it to be done?'

'Of course I do, what difference does it make? Who was responsible if you like. And that was her husband. I waited for the police to take some action, but when they didn't I thought I'd better do something about it myself. So I went along to The Bishop's Move and I found two people who had seen them talking together – Porson and Willard. This chap Porson's picture had been in the papers, and I showed them a copy of that. It wasn't difficult to get an identification, and they both knew Willard by sight.'

'I see. And what did you do then?'

'I found out who they were and where they lived.'

'And went to the police and told them that there was this

evidence ready and waiting for them?'

'Yes, that's what I did.'

'You see, Mr Eardley, that's all very clear but it does leave one big question-mark. What prompted you to go to The Bishop's Move in the first place? It wasn't a regular haunt of yours, was it?'

'Certainly not. I don't frequent such places.'

'Then what decided you to go there?'

'I knew Willard was in the habit of doing so, when he came over to take Jamie out. Laura had told me that.'

'It still doesn't explain why you should have thought there was evidence to be obtained there.'

'I knew he'd been drinking the second time Laura and I saw him together. I could smell it on his breath.'

'A dreadful indictment,' Maitland commented, wondering whether it was to be followed by Chris's theory – or was it something the prisoner himself had suggested? – that Eardley had hoped to find that Richard, in his cups, had been making open threats against his wife. 'Did my client tell you on that occasion that he'd just come from The Bishop's Move?'

'He didn't say, but . . . well, I thought it was worth a try.'

'A shot in the dark in fact.'

'Yes, that's it. I couldn't see Willard going free, and I'm not the sort of chap to take the law into my own hands.'

'Except by acting as an informer,' murmured counsel.

'My civic duty.'

'Very commendable. But you still haven't explained to us why you felt there was evidence to be obtained in that particular place.'

'Does it matter?'

'Yes, Mr Eardley, I think it does.' The quiet tone had gone, the words came sharply.

'It was just an idea I had.'

'You are going to tell us perhaps that you are psychic?' He was openly pressing the witness now and the scorn in his voice was apparent.

156

'No, I –' Eardley was looking wildly about him. 'I just felt –'

'I'm sure you did. But unless you are claiming some sort of divine revelation, there must have been a reason for that feeling. You would claim to be a reasonable man, I suppose.'

'It was Miss Hargreaves who suggested it,' said Eardley desperately.

'Indeed?'

'Miss Amanda Hargreaves, Laura's sister.'

'My lord.' Maitland turned to the judge. 'With your permission and my learned friend's goodwill I should like to go a little further into this matter. Miss Hargreaves's reasons –'

'Hearsay evidence, Mr Maitland?'

'It would be open to us to call the lady to speak for herself, my lord, but at a time when she is so distressed by her sister's death we – and I am sure my friend, Mr Anderson, is of the same mind – do not wish to do so. If your lordship will permit –'

Again Gilmour interrupted him. 'It seems a very small matter.'

'For my part, my lord, I have no objection,' Anderson put in. As well he might, Maitland considered; it was his own witness who was being given the opportunity of extracting himself from a pit he had dug himself.

'Very well.' The judge looked from one of them to the other, and then turned to the witness. 'Did you have some conversation with Miss Hargreaves on the subject?' he enquired.

The delay had obviously given Eardley a chance to arrange his thoughts. 'I did, my lord,' he said. 'I'd been thinking about where to start, and talking to Miss Hargreaves about it, because she was upset too and just as keen as I was to see justice done. And she said Willard must have arranged to meet Porson somewhere, and perhaps a pub where he was known to be an habitué would have been as good a place as any. So I went along at the time *he* used to

157

go –' he jerked his head in the direction of the man in the dock '– and sure enough I found what I wanted.'

'Thank you, Mr Eardley. Is that all you wanted to know, Mr Maitland?'

'It is, my lord.'

'It seems to me that Mr Eardley is to be congratulated on his good sense in following such excellent advice. Have you any further questions for him?'

'No, my lord. Unless Mr Anderson –?' But Anderson only shook his head. To Maitland's eye Counsel for the Prosecution was looking half bewildered, half aggrieved, but he rose to his feet and called for his next witness calmly enough.

There followed Richard's landlady, whom Maitland allowed to go without questioning. Nor did he question Anderson's final witness, the man who had served the divorce papers on Richard Willard. After that Anderson declared his case closed, the judge glanced at the clock on the wall of the courtroom and to everyone's relief decided to adjourn for the weekend. 'That will give you plenty of time to prepare your opening address, Mr Maitland,' he added, and Antony couldn't decide whether it was courtesy that prompted the remark or a rather unkind pleasure in anticipation of the difficulty he would probably have in doing so.

Once the judge had gone he did not linger. 'Go and see our client, Chris,' he commanded.

'There's nothing very cheerful to say to him,' Chris objected. 'We didn't get anywhere with Eardley. I can't think why you didn't insist on calling Amanda Hargreaves. She might have denied giving him that advice. As it is –'

'I got as far as I expected with Eardley, but . . . no, don't try to cheer Willard up, it might be too unkind. I just don't want him to think we're neglecting him.'

'Aren't you coming too?'

'No, I'm going to see Grandma.'

'Oh, for heaven's sake!' He looked hard at his friend for a moment. 'Shall I come with you?' he asked.

'No, I think this time I'd better go alone. There's

something I want to ask her and she may talk more willingly to a stranger.'

'You're hardly a stranger after all this time,' Chris objected.

'No . . . I meant, when it comes to what she always calls scurrilous talk she might be more willing to open up to someone who doesn't live in Arkenshaw. Bear with me, Chris,' he added, seeing his friend hesitate. 'Will you ring Jenny to tell her I shan't be coming home tonight.'

'Yes, of course I will. I'll take your briefcase too and you can pick it up later. You know what time dinner is, and there'll be plenty if you want to join us.'

'I will if I can. I'm sorry, Chris, I really am sorry but this is urgent. Willard's going rapidly to pieces. I – I know how he feels, being shut up. I don't want to torture him with hope if there isn't any, but if there's anything at all –' He broke off then and added more formally, 'I'm treating you very badly, but perhaps in the long run you'll forgive me.'

II

The taxi driver who took him up to Old Peel Farm was friendly and talkative. 'Will you be wanting me to wait for you?' he asked as they approached their destination.

'I'm afraid I don't know how long I shall be.'

'It's a bit out of the way,' said the driver cheerfully. 'But there's a housing estate now at the end of the lane and a place where I can get a cuppa, which wouldn't be unwelcome. Suppose I give you their telephone number, then you can call me when you want me.'

That seemed a good idea, and Antony agreed to it. The wind that greeted him when he got out of the car seemed colder than ever, but the door was opened by Grandma herself rather more quickly than usual after his knock, which he took to mean that she'd been already on her feet. 'It's you, is it?' she greeted him. 'I didn't expect to see you this

159

evening.' She added, taking his coat.

Antony knew better than to answer immediately, except by way of greeting. Any loitering in the hall was frowned on, and he pressed the switch to extinguish the light there and followed her into the warm kitchen. 'Didn't the stars warn you I'd be coming?' he asked then, smiling at her.

'Don't you go making fun of things you don't understand,' she told him. 'A bad day for Cancer and I'd have told you that if you'd asked me. And from the looks of you,' she added, eyeing him more closely, 'I'm right about that.'

That day there were no tea things set out – Grandma would have had hers already – but the table cloth had been laid and crockery and cutlery seemed to be waiting for arrangement. 'Just getting Fred's supper,' said Grandma, following her visitor's glance.

'You're busy, and I shouldn't be bothering you.'

'Nay, there's nowt for me to do but to get out pots. I've a lass comes in most days now, and she leaves it ready.' She glanced down at her hands as she spoke, and suddenly he felt that she couldn't have paid him a nicer compliment. She was a very independent old lady and it must have cost her a good deal to admit to the need for help. 'You look as if you could do with something stronger than tea,' she added, surprising him. 'There's a whisky in t'sideboard cupboard, Fred likes a drop occasionally. You'd best help yourself. Nay, get on with it, there's a good lad,' she added as he hesitated, and crossed the room to seat herself regally in her favourite high-backed Windsor chair.

There were glasses in the cupboard too. Antony did as he was bid, went out to the scullery for water and returned to sit at the other side of the hearth. He knew better than to have asked her to join him, and, though he didn't like drinking alone, the scotch – a blend he wasn't familiar with – was very welcome. He took a sip and then looked up at her, sitting with the glass cradled between his hands. 'I expect you know why I'm here, Grandma,' he said.

'Nay, how should I know a thing like that?'

160

'Because you're one of the wisest people I know.' He laughed rather shamefacedly. 'I always come to you when I'm in trouble, don't I?'

'Personal trouble?' she asked, frowning.

'Not this time. But the prosecution have finished presenting their case, and I've nothing to answer it with except my client's denial of guilt. Which in the circumstances I don't think will convince anybody.'

'You've lost cases before,' she said. 'Not here in Arkenshaw, I know, but it isn't the end of the world.'

'Not for me.'

'Taking all the world's troubles on your shoulders as usual,' said Grandma severely. 'If I've told you once –'

'Yes, I know, it doesn't even help the people I'm worrying about,' said Antony. 'Is Inspector Duckett still angry with Chris and Star?' he asked inconsequently.

'It's along of Jim Ryder's death,' said Grandma, as though the matter still required explanation. 'I told him they've a right to their opinion of their friend, and I think he's beginning to see it isn't as if Chris was deliberately trying to shield Jim's murderer.'

'When are you expecting him home?'

She looked up at the clock on the mantelshelf. ''appen in about half an hour,' she said. 'We've time to talk if that's what you came for.'

'What else?'

'You might be looking for sympathy but I daresay you know better than that. You'll get none from me.' As usual her forthright manner was having the effect of raising his spirits from the depths to which they had plunged.

'It's just as well I wasn't expecting any then, isn't it?' he asked in a teasing tone, and grinned at her unrepentantly when his levity brought a frown to her face. 'Will you tell me something, Grandma?' he added more seriously.

''appen I will, and 'appen I won't.'

Nothing for it but to try. 'I've been thinking about the talk we had last week,' said Antony. 'I thought at the time . . . but

161

when you talked about *her end being bitter as wormwood* you weren't thinking of Laura, were you?'

There was a long silence. 'It was true about her, wasn't it?' said Grandma.

'Yes, but . . . it isn't like you to avoid giving a direct answer.'

'If you will have it then . . . no.'

'Who was it?'

The eagerness in his tone was a mistake. 'Why should I tell thee that then, lad?' she asked, and the use of the second person singular told him that she was deeply disturbed. 'Never one for making trouble, I wasn't.'

'Grandma!' he said pleadingly.

'Give me one good reason then why I should tell you.'

'Because . . . oh, because I've come to believe that Star and Chris are right about Richard Willard. He didn't arrange for his wife's death, he isn't responsible for what happened to Jim Ryder. And if he's found guilty, it won't only be his life that's ruined, but that of the very nice woman whom he wants to marry, and of his son Jamie too. Jamie's very nearly the same age as Tommy was when you took him in,' he told her, as though that might add to the persuasiveness of what he had said.

She looked at him closely for a long moment. 'Are you sure of that, Mr Maitland?'

He would have liked to lie to her. 'As sure as one can be of anything in this uncertain world,' he said, and was relieved when her rather grim look relaxed into a smile

'Aye, that's just like you,' she said. 'Will you tell me something else then?'

'I suppose I must.'

'What gave you the idea he was innocent? Was it because our Star and Chris believed it?'

'I think I told you, Grandma, I have great faith in Star's judgement.'

'Then you persuaded yourself because they're your friends and you wanted to believe them?'

162

'No.' The word came out more sharply than he had intended. 'I didn't – I hope I didn't persuade myself of anything. I came to believe that someone else is guilty and I think it was the same person you were wondering about when we spoke before. But you didn't want to cause trouble for somebody else if Willard was guilty.'

'Tell me then, who do *you* think arranged all this?'

'Amanda Hargreaves.'

Grandma gave a long sigh. 'If you're right –' she said, and didn't attempt to complete the sentence.

'I am right, Grandma! And she was the person who came into your mind as a possibility – wasn't she? – if only you hadn't believed so firmly that the police were right about Willard.'

'I wasn't sure, think on. I'm still not sure, come to that. 'appen you'd better tell me –'

Antony in his turn glanced up at the clock. 'The Inspector will be here in a moment,' he said. 'Won't you take my word for it for the present, Grandma, and tell me what's in your mind. Then I can talk to him and give him my own reasons.'

Again she hesitated. 'It was along of her job,' she said at last.

'Her job? Oh lord, what a fool I've been! Is it – was it – something that might have enabled her to get in touch with Porson?'

'She's a newspaper reporter and works in Northdean,' said Grandma. 'Or did until she came back to look after Jamie. Susan Hargreaves used to talk about her, of course, and she was a bit upset at first when she was given the job of reporting on criminal cases. Not the sort of thing a lady should be doing, she thought, but there! they'll be up to anything, the lasses these days and afterwards even Susan had to admit it was interesting, the things Amanda'd tell her. It isn't very much to go on,' she added apologetically, 'but it did make me wonder.'

'What a fool I was!' said Maitland again. 'The answer to the biggest puzzle of all, just waiting for the right question to

163

be asked. But it doesn't quite explain . . . do you know Amanda, Grandma?'

'Only through her mother's talk.'

'Her mother wouldn't be likely to say anything against her.'

'No, but she's sometimes not very wise, Susan isn't. She always said what gentle girls Laura and Amanda were, but Laura, I know for a fact, could be stuborn when she wanted, and it always seemed to me that Amanda had a hard streak in her, just from hearing her mother talk. Which was why I wondered at her staying to take charge of Jamie, instead of letting Henry and his wife do it when they'd have given their eyes to have the boy with them. Amanda was always a lively one, Susan said, and I'm sure looking after him would cramp her style.'

'But *why*, Grandma? That's another question you may be able to answer for me. Was it just the money?'

'Her mother's money, you mean? No, I don't think it was that. If Henry and Maria made a fight for it, do you think Amanda would get custody of Jamie?'

'No, but . . . I can't think of anything else,' he admitted. 'Something that made her hate Richard as well as Laura.'

'If she did it – and you haven't told me yet why you think so, Mr Maitland – but if she did it, it was jealousy, black, wicked jealousy.'

'She told me she didn't even know Eardley. She couldn't have been jealous just because Laura was getting married again.'

'There you go, jumping to conclusions as usual,' said Grandma, so that he thought suddenly of his uncle and his frequent strictures of much the same nature. 'Go back thirteen years to the time Richard Willard joined the repertory here and got to know the Hargreaves sisters. Susan told me she thought he was going to ask Amanda to marry him, he met her first, but then he up and married Laura to everyone's surprise. It wasn't just Susan I heard about that from, there was a lot of talk in the town. Something else

164

Susan told me, she didn't want Laura to turn her husband out, but she said Amanda thought it was the only thing to do. So I wouldn't wonder if she'd been putting ideas into her sister's head all along . . . envy, hatred, and all uncharitableness,' she added severely.

'That would explain . . . but could anyone hold a grudge like that all these years?'

'Some women could. You were going to say it would explain why she wanted Richard to be blamed.'

'But why *now*, after all this time?' But even as he posed the question the answer came to him. 'I suppose it was because for the first time an opportunity came to have it done in complete safety to herself. Sykes – you remember Superintendent Sykes, Grandma?'

'I remember Bill, but it's a long time since I saw him.'

'His real name is Marmaduke,' said Antony, for some reason feeling he should put the record straight. 'He told me that some of what he called Porson's associates had been involved in jobs outside London. That some of them had been caught. If I phone him he'll tell me if there was a case in Northdean recently. That would just about clinch matters, wouldn't it?'

'Unless you believe in coincidences.'

'Coincidences happen,' said Antony, thinking of an afternoon the previous October when a whole crowd of coincidences had landed together on Sir Nicholas's doorstep, to his uncle's great annoyance. 'Still I don't think in this case . . . the question is, Grandma, what do I do now?'

'You said you were going to talk to Fred.'

'Yes, and I still think that's what I'd better do, but wouldn't it be nice to get an answer to that question from Sykes first?'

Grandma smiled at him. 'You're thinking our Fred's not got a very credulous disposition,' she said.

'What Yorkshireman has?' asked Antony rhetorically. 'Don't you think on the whole, Grandma, that's the best idea?'

'You could phone from here.'

'Yes, but I imagine he'll be on his way home at the moment, and if I hang around too long I'll find myself explaining myself to Inspector Duckett before I'm really ready.'

'All right then, but if you tell me these reasons of yours quickly 'appen I could prepare your way a bit.'

''appen you could an' all, Grandma,' said Antony, smiling at her. 'You're altogether too good to me, you know. And I can tell you in just about two minutes, but I'm afraid when you hear what I have to say you'll think I had a cheek approaching you tonight.'

'Never mind that, you'd best tell me.'

'All right then.' He thought about it for a moment, frowning. 'I had just one talk with Amanda Hargreaves, and I came away from it with an uncomfortable feeling, though I couldn't put my finger on what was wrong. My doubts about Willard's guilt – which I have to admit started because of what I'd heard from Star and Chris – began to crystallise from that moment. So naturally I gave our interview some thought.'

'Well?' she prompted when he hesitated.

'Such small things,' he said again. 'She seemed to be talking to me quite freely, but she didn't really tell me anything. And I was quite sure, on reflection, that she'd been deliberately trying to steer me away from suspecting anyone but Willard. I couldn't blame her for believing him guilty, of course, but this was rather different. And she agreed when I asked her not to disillusion Jamie, but heaven knows what she'd been telling him and heaven knows whether she kept her word. You see until he talked to me he obviously was afraid his father was guilty, and I don't think he'd have reached that conclusion alone. He's probably read hundreds of books where the hero was wrongly accused; that would be bound to be the first thing to come into his head.'

'Aye, it would that.'

'And then when I was leaving, Amanda told me not to

166

forget that Jamie was relying on me. That sounds innocent enough, doesn't it? But I'm pretty sure she knew it would worry me, and that she said it out of malice.'

'As you say, Mr Maitland, little enough,' said Grandma nodding. 'If I didn't know you –'

'That's not quite all, Grandma. She deliberately misled me about Jamie's future financial position. But I don't suppose I'd have dared to approach you again at all if I hadn't got a sort of confirmation of what I was beginning to believe in court today. I was cross-examining Lionel Eardley, the man Laura wanted to marry after she'd divorced Richard. Which reminds me, Chris is quite sure I believe Eardley's guilty, I'll have to put him right about that.'

'What was this confirmation then?'

'If part of the plot was to see that Richard was blamed for the murder, it was essential that the police should find out about the talk he had with Porson at The Bishop's Move. Amanda knew Richard's habits when he came to visit Jamie, and could quite well have arranged the encounter in the first place, but then the police's visit there, which could only have been routine from their point of view, didn't turn anything up. But Eardley admitted that he'd gone to the pub at Amanda's suggestion, and at noon on Sunday because she thought a public house would have been a very likely place for Richard to have arranged to meet this man. I shouldn't be surprised if she'd encouraged him to do a bit of detective work in the first place when Richard wasn't arrested immediately – he's a spiteful chap himself and wouldn't need much encouragement, but that's only guesswork.'

Grandma made no direct comment but began to struggle to her feet. 'You get along then,' she said. 'Do you need to telephone for a cab?' Anthony explained the arrangement he had made. 'Well, you know where the phone is,' she told him. 'And I agree with you it's best this way. I'll have got our Fred properly softened up by the time you get back.'

III

When he got back to the hotel he thought that with any luck Sykes would have arrived home, and as soon as he'd got the detective's private number from directory inquiries – he'd used it a number of times in the past, but not often enough to fix it in his memory – he put the call through. It was Mrs Sykes who answered, but the Superintendent came in while she was talking to him. 'One of Porson's associates involved in a case in Northdean?' he said incredulously when Maitland had put his question. 'What on earth put that into your head?'

'The person I suspect was a crime reporter on one of the newspapers there. I've only just found that out. It could have been how she got in touch with Porson.'

'She?'

'The victim's sister,' said Antony impatiently. 'What about it, Sykes?'

'You're quite right, there was such a case, two or three months ago.'

'I knew it!'

'Now, Mr Maitland, it's obvious you know something that the police don't. Do you mean to use it in court?'

'Not unless I must.'

'If that means you're going to take matters into your own hands . . . don't do anything so foolish.'

'Don't worry, I only meant I'd have to do what I could in court if your colleagues up here won't listen to me. You see, I've just had another thought – something else that should have occurred to me sooner – I think I know where Porson is.'

'Mr Maitland –'

'Yes, Superintendent?'

'What are you going to do?' Uncharacteristically, Sykes almost howled the words.

'I'm going back to Old Peel Farm to try to convince

168

Inspector Duckett first. If I can get him on my side, that should go a long way towards persuading the detective branch that my story's at least worth looking into. I'm going to ring off now, because there's no time to be wasted, but I'll be eternally grateful –'

'You think Porson may get away?'

'No, not just yet. Not until the hue and cry's died down a bit. But I don't want to waste any time all the same; the trouble is my client's got a touch of claustrophobia.'

He had just replaced the receiver and was wondering how long he should give Grandma to work on that very stubborn, if not positively pig-headed man, Inspector Duckett, when the phone rang sharply again. Afterwards he was to wonder why it should have immediately infected him with a sense of urgency, by far the most likely thing was that it was Jenny or Sir Nicholas trying to get hold of him after receiving his message through Chris. The fact remained that as he picked the receiver up again he was conscious of a sense of foreboding, which the frantic voice that reached him certainly did nothing to dispel.

'Is that you, Mr Maitland?' Antony acknowledged the fact. 'It's Jamie . . . Jamie Willard. I don't know what to do.'

'Take a deep breath, Jamie, and tell me what's wrong.'

'There's no time. Can you do something . . . please! There's a man here, I think he's been living –' The frantic words broke off suddenly as though a hand had been clapped over the boy's mouth. There was a moment of dead silence and then the receiver at the other end of the line was very gently replaced.

No time for hesitation. No time to remember the promises he had made to Jenny, and Sykes, and everybody else. Maitland dialled the Ducketts' number immediately, and was relieved when he was answered by Inspector Duckett's voice after only a brief interval. 'I don't know if Grandma's had time to talk to you yet, Inspector,' he said, without wasting time on even the briefest greeting, 'but will you take my word for something? I know where Porson is, he's been

169

hiding out at Laura Willard's house, probably in the garage. Could you get in touch with Superintendent Morrison, or whoever the right person is, and come out there right away? I'm going to get hold of Chris and go on ahead. Something seems to have happened to Jamie Willard, which I think means Porson's left his hiding place, so you won't need a search warrant.'

'Reet.' The Inspector was not a man to waste words. 'Grandma started to tell me some rigmarole, but there'll be time for that later.'

'Good.' As soon as he had the line again he phoned Chris. 'No time for explanations,' he said. 'Drop everything and come and pick me up at the hotel.'

There had been times in the past when he had fumed at the cautious approach a Yorkshireman very often takes to life, but today he had no complaint to make. Chris drew up at the door of the hotel almost as soon as he had reached the front door himself, and started the car again almost as soon as Maitland had got in beside him. 'I hope I'm going in the right direction,' he said mildly after a moment. 'Where are we going?'

'To see Amanda Hargreaves.'

'All right then, full speed ahead,' said Chris. The odd thing was that he showed no surprise at all at his companion's sudden decisiveness. But he did add, as he sent the car forward at what for him was a quite unprecedented speed, 'You can explain what we're up to as we go.'

Antony obliged. 'I quite thought, you know,' said Chris when he had finished, 'that Eardley was the guilty party, and that you believed that too.'

'There have been times when I wondered about him, of course, but after seeing him in court . . . well, if you want my opinion, Chris, he was too obviously venomous to be guilty.'

'You said Amanda –'

'She took every opportunity of emphasising the likelihood of Richard's being responsible, but she was extremely subtle about it.'

'Well, what do we do now?'

'*We* don't do anything. You stop the car well down the street and wait for the police to arrive.'

'Oh no, I don't. If you think I'm going to let you get out of my sight this time –'

'And if you think I'm going to face Star and young Tony later with the news of your demise . . . I don't mean to go barging in regardless, Chris, but someone's got to look out for Jamie. Heaven knows what's happened to him by now.'

'Then we'll reconnoitre together,' said Chris firmly, and something in his tone prevented Maitland from arguing the matter any further. 'How would you interpret that telephone call of Jamie's?'

'To begin with you must remember that Porson had no idea the local police were on his tail. He isn't known in Yorkshire, and it was only pure chance that he was seen leaving King's Cross. So he'd be expecting to be able to make his getaway in his own good time, with nobody knowing who was responsible for the shooting. But when Ryder tackled him – we don't know exactly what happened, but Porson probably realised that he was a member of the force, or at any rate was afraid he might be, which would mean they were looking for *him*, not for some unknown gunman. So the only thing he could do was disappear for a while, until he could get in touch with someone who'd help him make a complete getaway.'

'That sounds reasonable.'

'I don't think it's surprising he thought of the Willard place first of all. He'd know Amanda was arriving that evening, and if you remember she was alone in the house for the rest of the night because Jamie was already in bed next door. There'd be visits from the police, of course, but I expect he was pretty sure of being able to find somewhere to conceal himself. He may not even have known that Laura had a son, but in any case I daresay he felt it was up to his principal to suggest something. It's quite a large house, ridiculously so for two people, and the grounds are large too and the garage positively enormous. I didn't notice it particularly when I took Jamie home, but I wouldn't be surprised to find that there's a room above, or at least some storage space. Porson could bed down there quite comfortably and Amanda could keep him provided with food and drink. Not an ideal situation for either of them, but the best they could do in the circumstances.'

'So you think he's been there almost exactly a month now without Jamie knowing anything about it.'

'Why should he know? He isn't old enough to drive, so there's no question of his going to take the car out and, as long as Amanda was careful in the matter of provisions, I don't see why he should have suspected anything. After all, even at twelve years old he probably goes to bed considerably before she does. But today – I'm guessing at this stage but I don't think I can be very far wrong – something must have alerted the boy. If the garage is used for storage he may have gone there to look for something and heard a footstep above. Porson, who must be a cool customer but can't help but be a bit on edge by now, may have realised Jamie had grown suspicious and followed him to the house, heard him telephoning, and stopped him in the easiest and quickest way by clapping his hand over his mouth. After that . . . I don't like to think of what may have happened after that, Chris.'

'We'll soon know.' He pulled the car up three doors away from the Willard house and was out and on the pavement before Maitland himself could emerge. 'Do you remember,' he said, 'the time you gave me the slip and went round to the printing works and confronted Frank Findlater? I've never quite forgiven you for that.'

'It wasn't of malice aforethought, and you put your time to better advantage,' said Maitland mildly. 'You proposed to Star.'

'So I did.' Chris grinned at him. 'So long as you understand,' he said, 'that I'm not getting left out of things this time.'

'Come along then, but for goodness' sake don't make any more noise than you can help.'

Chris, obediently playing follow my leader, was amused by Antony's cautious approach. It was quite dark by now and even in their leafless state the trees shadowed the drive. Maitland went up softly, treading on the grass verge, then paused for a moment to get his bearings. The drawing room where he had talked to Amanda was to the right of the front door, and though the curtains were close drawn he could see the faintest crack of light. On so cold a night there was no chance of an open window, but there was just the possibility that in the emergency that must have arisen one or other of the conspirators might have left the front door unlatched.

'We'll try that,' he said quietly as Chris came up beside him, and Chris nodded as though in perfect comprehension and followed him on tiptoe across the wide expanse of the drive. Antony's sense of humour was not quite proof against the ridiculous sight they must have presented, even in his present state of anxiety, but they reached the front door without incident. When he tried the knob cautiously it yielded not an inch, but here, close against the wall, he could see where the curtain around the bay window had been carelessly drawn, probably in haste to conceal what lay within. Whoever had done it had pulled too hard, so that at least an inch of the window was left uncovered, and through it they could see a narrow strip of the room. There was no sign of Jamie, but by chance Amanda Hargreaves was in full view, and facing her the man whose likeness had been circulated throughout the country, Edwin Porson. They seemed to be arguing, though no words were audible.

Antony turned to his companion, still speaking softly. 'I'm going in,' he said. 'It would really be helpful if you stayed outside to tell the police what's happening.'

'If I know my revered father-in-law,' said Chris in an equally muted voice, 'he won't need any telling. What are you going to do, break the window?'

'Nothing so common. I'm going to ring the bell like a

173

civilised person. And if you insist on coming in with me, Chris, for heaven's sake be ready if I can create an opportunity for action, but don't try anything unless you're sure. That chap's dangerous.'

'Antony –' He would have liked to add, 'you're scared yourself, aren't you?' but the words stuck in his throat. Maitland, who had never gone into a dangerous situation in his life without realising its possibilities fully, gave him an understanding look, but did not try further to dissuade him.

'In the meantime,' he said, 'keep your eye on that crack, there's a good chap, and tell me what's happening.'

Far in the depths of the house they could hear the jangle of the bell. 'They've stopped talking and are staring at each other,' said Chris. And a moment later, 'I think he's told her to find out who it is.'

'They must have a very good idea,' Maitland began, but the door was pulled open before he could complete the thought.

'Oh, Mr Maitland,' said Amanda. She could hardly be surprised, but she was putting on a good show. 'I wasn't expecting to see you again until after the trial at least.'

'As a matter of fact,' said Antony, 'it's Jamie we wanted to see. Aren't you going to let us in? You'll get cold standing there without a coat.' He was edging forward as he spoke with Chris on his heels, so that she really had no alternative but to back away. As soon as they were both in the hall Chris shut the front door and leaned back against it.

'Was it you Jamie called?' said Amanda. 'I didn't know who it could have been. A friend of mine came here earlier in the evening and it seemed to upset him. He's not quite himself, you know, at the moment, but I'm sure you'll understand that. You were so understanding when you were here before.'

'Yes, he did call me. This is Mr Conway, by the way, your sister's husband's solicitor. I can't remember whether you've met. Anyway, now we're here we should very much like to see the boy.'

'I'm afraid he's gone to bed.'

'So early?'

'I told you he was upset, I thought it was the best thing to do.'

'Well, in that case, perhaps we could see the visitor you mentioned.'

That brought a quick frown. 'He left some time ago.'

'Don't deliberately misunderstand me, Miss Hargreaves. I mean what our American cousins would call your house guest. Or would it be more correct to say garage guest? Edwin Porson,' he amplified.

'I don't know what you're talking about.' Her voice had taken on a little shrillness now. 'You force your way in here, and make some monstrous suggestion –'

'You may as well let them in,' a man's voice interrupted from the doorway of the drawing room. 'It was a good try, Amanda, but we're going to have to think of something better to get rid of them.'

'Don't you dare to call me Amanda.' She turned on him furiously. 'If you'd gone instead of arguing –'

'Your position might have improved, but mine would certainly have worsened. As it is . . . you see, Mr Maitland, if you try to start anything in the nature of a rough house it's Jamie who'll get hurt.' His voice was deep and curiously soothing, a tall man with straight sleek hair and a face that had probably been good-looking before the scar disfigured it. His left hand was across Jamie's mouth and he had pulled the boy back close against his chest. His right hand held an automatic pistol rammed against the boy's side. 'Stalemate, I think.' he said mockingly.

Over the restraining hand Jamie's eyes met Maitland's beseechingly, but there was no time now for reassurance. 'For the moment,' Antony agreed. And then, 'Mr Edwin Porson, I presume.'

'The same.'

'You'd be very well advised to drop your weapon.'

'Why should I? One of the things I know about you, Mr

Maitland, is that you're a cripple, not much good in a scrap any longer, are you? And even if your young friend – Conway did you say his name was? – is feeling impetuous, I doubt if he really wants to see the boy killed any more than you do.'

'Do you?'

'Why certainly. And as things have turned out, I'm afraid it will be rather a wholesale slaughter. Miss Hargreaves' – his tone gave the formal title a satiric sound – 'and I were just discussing what is best to do . . . afterwards.'

'It's very simple really,' Maitland told him. 'Let the boy go and get the hell out of here. I don't think the police will be very far behind us.'

'That's another thing I've heard about you, that you're a good talker. Do you really expect me to believe that?'

'Whether you do or not is really immaterial. It happens to be true.'

'Come now, they're convinced of Willard's guilt. Why should they suspect anything so unlikely?'

'Because I told them who your principal was and I told them you were here and I told them Jamie's life was in danger.' And if that wasn't strictly true it was near enough.

Surprisingly Porson laughed. 'I find that very hard to believe,' he said. 'Are you any fonder of making a fool of yourself than the next man? You wouldn't make a statement to them with nothing to back it up and if you did they wouldn't believe you.'

'Are you so sure of that?' Maitland was fighting off a feeling of unreality. He couldn't quite remember now what he had expected Porson to be like, but certainly he hadn't anticipated an educated man; and now he was wondering, rather wildly, what could have led him into a line of business where in the nature of things he must spend so much of his time among people with whom he had nothing in common. 'Miss Hargreaves may have told you that Chris Conway here is the son-in-law of one of the senior members of the local police force.'

'And at odds with him over the question of his defending

Richard,' said Amanda. 'I may have been living quietly but I'm not altogether cut off from the local gossip, Mr Maitland.'

'I think however it might be in your own interests – both of you – to hear what I have to say,' said Antony. 'Why don't we go into the drawing room?' he added as casually as he could. 'Then you could let Jamie go, and both of you would be more comfortable.'

'And have him yell his head off?'

'I doubt if anyone would hear him. In any case, Jamie's quite intelligent enough to know that wouldn't be advisable, not so long as you're armed. Aren't you, Jamie?'

Behind the restraining hand Jamie achieved a sort of gurgling sound. 'There, you see,' said Maitland. 'He agrees with me.'

'Have it your own way then.' He was probably as tired of holding Jamie as the boy was of being held. 'But understand, all of you, that one false move and it's the boy that gets it.' He twisted Jamie round to face him. 'Do *you* understand?' he demanded.

Jamie noded dumbly. 'I told you,' said Amanda harshly. 'I don't want the boy hurt.'

'That, my dear lady, was before these gentlemen arrived. You must see that their coming has radically changed the situation. Before that your point of view had a certain validity, though of course I didn't agree with you. But now –' He broke off and gave Jamie a shove in the direction of the drawing-room door. 'By all means let us make ourselves comfortable,' he said. 'Perhaps you will go ahead, Mr Maitland, and you too, Mr Conway.'

Antony obeyed the instructions, taking as much time as he could over it without appearing to be loitering. His mind was racing frantically, how long would it be before his talk with Inspector Duckett could bear fruit in the shape of reinforcements? Some time, he was afraid, there'd be explanations to make and some persuasion to do, and he and Chris had got here pretty quickly. Old Peel Farm was on the other side of the town and a fair distance from the centre. If a telephone call to the detective branch had been sufficient . . . but he couldn't rely on that. The only thing to be thankful for was that Porson appeared to feel no sense of urgency. If he'd believed that first statement that the police were on their way and made off himself that would have been all to the good; as it was their best hope was to persuade him that it had been a lie.

The room was just as he had seen it before, the very essence of suburban respectability. Laura Willard, he thought suddenly, must have been a dull woman, but that was hardly useful knowledge at this point. For all his talk of making themselves comfortable he had no intention of sitting down if that could possibly be avoided. Instead of making for the fireplace, therefore, he went towards the window, taking Jamie's arm and dragging him in the same direction.

When he turned it was with his left arm casually but reassuringly draped round the boy's shoulder. Chris followed his example and arranged himself on his other side. Behind them was a table with a fine assortment of house plants and, at the end of it, an aspidistra on a tall stand which Antony felt he wouldn't have believed if he hadn't seen it with his own eyes. Beyond that again was the bay window with its heavy curtains. Porson, holding the gun now with a studied negligence that didn't deceive any of them, was standing about five feet away, but Amanda seated herself on the arm of one of the easy chairs that circled the fireplace.

'On the whole it's a pity you saw through my little deception,' said Maitland. 'It would have saved a lot of bother.' Was he going too far, would it be too much for them to swallow? But a man who had lived as Edwin Porson had lived couldn't by any stretch of the imagination be classed with the rank and file of humanity. There was one thing, however, that men – or women – who went in for a life of crime seemed to have in common . . . vanity. And as he

178

watched the gunman's face he thought with a certain, well-concealed exultation that he'd been right about that. Porson was quite satisfied with his own judgement of the situation and quite content to let matters ride for at least a little while longer. If he could keep him talking . . .

'That's to look at matters from a purely selfish point of view, Mr Maitland,' Porson was saying.

'I suppose it is,' Antony acknowledged. 'It would be interesting to know though what you and Miss Hargreaves were arguing about when we arrived.'

'Whether to kill the boy,' said Porson negligently.

'I'm surprised you should have troubled to argue about that. I gather from something that was said just now that it was Miss Hargreaves who objected. I don't quite see,' he added, turning to the woman, 'why, having arranged for your sister's death, you should object to one more killing.'

'Not on humanitarian grounds, I assure you,' said Porson before Amanda could speak. 'Such an action would naturally have been followed by my immediate departure, and she didn't feel she had the strength to dispose of the body in any permanent way. I was trying to persuade her that if I tied her up loosely before I left the police might easily be duped by the tale of an intruder. She could even have described me without any harm being done. I should have preferred to stay here another couple of days, but my arrangements for leaving the country are almost complete, and my friends, I am sure, can find me a safe hiding-place for that short length of time.'

'I think I'm being stupid,' said Antony. 'You are, if you'll forgive me for saying so, easily recognisable, so it would have been quite reasonable for Miss Hargreaves to disclaim all knowledge of you and still describe you to the police. But without incriminating herself how could she have explained your coming here, and what you had done?'

'Ah, that was the beauty of the whole idea. Revenge,' said Porson.

'I still don't understand.' He felt Jamie shiver and

179

tightened his arm a little.

'And I have always heard you were an intelligent man, Mr Maitland. Her story would have put the final touch to the case against Richard Willard, which it was part of our agreement to promote. She would have said that I had admitted to her that Willard had hired me, that I was resentful because I blamed him for the police finding out that I was still in Arkenshaw, and also because, through his ineptitude in getting himself arrested, I'd never been paid for my services.'

'That's very neat,' said Antony, doing his best to infuse an admiring tone into his voice. 'And what was Miss Hargreaves's objection?'

'I haven't had time to explain the full beauty of the scheme to her. She was concerned that Jamie's murder might mean that she too would have to disappear, whereas she's very anxious that her life should go on as before. But she'd have seen the sense of what I was saying in time, wouldn't you, Amanda?'

This time she didn't protest at the use of her Christian name. 'I suppose I should,' she acknowledged, 'but the situation has changed now. Since you're so clever,' she went on rather bitterly, 'what do you propose?'

'I'm afraid there's nothing for it but wholesale slaughter. It's a pity really, I've always rather despised the kind of thug who carries a handgun and uses it.'

'While your speciality is a rifle,' said Antony.

'Exactly, at any range you care to name. It's an exhilarating feeling and there's some artistry about it, I'm sure you can see that. Whereas . . . don't delude yourselves, I shan't miss at this range with this rather degraded object, but I should much prefer –'

Antony interrupted him. 'And what about you when all of this has taken place, Miss Hargreaves?' he asked.

'Yes, what about me?' The question was addressed to Porson, but again it was Maitland who replied.

'I don't think you'd quite get away with the first story that

Mr Porson suggested to explain why Mr Conway and I are here,' he pointed out. 'We're Richard Willard's lawyers, and once the police got round to wondering what we were doing here I think it wouldn't be long before they stumbled on the truth. You'd have achieved half your plan, your sister would be dead, but your brother-in-law would be acquitted.'

'If Jamie were dead his father would suffer for it for the rest of his life,' said Amanda, in a strangely matter-of-fact tone. 'I know him well enough for that.'

'But what about you? If you're considering staying here with three corpses on the premises, you'll probably end up in prison yourself, with no chance of things returning to normal for you.'

'I'd have to go away,' she said doubtfully.

'Which you don't want to do?'

'No.'

'What can't be cured must be endured, as my old grandmother used to say,' Edwin Porson put in.

'Yes, but I don't think Miss Hargreaves is going to enjoy being a fugitive,' said Antony. 'Have you thought what it would be like?' he asked Amanda. 'No money, no identity, always wondering when you might be recognised, always looking over your shoulder –'

'What else can I do? If we let you go –'

'Mr Porson thinks no one would believe us if we told the truth about what happened.'

'It's a question of time,' said Porson. 'Given long enough you might succeed, so I'm afraid there's no question of allowing you to live to tell the tale. As for Amanda –'

'Yes, what about her? Do your plans include her'?'

'They'll have to, won't they?'

'There you see, Miss Hargreaves, your future is assured. I believe the phrase "a gangster's moll" is rather out of date, but I'm afraid I don't know the current one. Anyway, it's descriptive enough, and that's what you'll be. One of two, as I understand it. It seems he already has a wife.'

'I won't, I won't!'

'It seems you have a mutiny on your hands, Mr Porson. But before these melancholy events take place would you mind telling me, Miss Hargreaves, exactly why you let yourself in for all of this?'

'Because I loved Richard once and she took him away from me. So I've hated them both ever since, and over the years . . . he was successful and happy, at least that's what Laura told me. And she was content enough living here with Jamie. And then she was going to be married again. But I still wouldn't have done anything if the perfect opportunity hadn't seemed to come along, when I interviewed that friend of his' – she made a slight scornful gesture in Porson's direction – 'after he was acquitted in Northdean on a charge of extortion. It was quite obvious he was guilty, only the jury were too stupid to see it, but he didn't mind talking to me – showing off – because he knew he couldn't be tried again for the same thing, and I couldn't print anything that might amount to libel. And one thing led to another, and gradually I realised that here was the chance I'd been waiting for, and at exactly the right time, because Laura had written to me about the trouble she was having with Richard.'

'Was it worth it?'

She closed her eyes for a moment. 'Yes, I think it was,' she said. 'Do you know what it is to be eaten up by jealousy, Mr Maitland? It was like coming to life again when I knew Laura was dead, and then I told that stupid man Eardley where to look for the evidence against Richard. Oh yes, it was worth it.'

'And what was in it for you, Mr Porson?'

'Money,' he said simply. 'A good deal of it as the plan involved my leaving the country.'

'Ah, yes, the plot against Willard involved your identity becoming known. How did you intend to arrange that, Miss Hargreaves?'

'A phone call, an anonymous letter. I'd have pretended to be someone with a grudge against him.'

'A woman of infinite resource and sagacity,' said Antony

182

admiringly. 'It must have been a hefty payment. In advance, I hope.'

'What else? She told me she'd been saving up for years.'

'But does the amount you've been paid really recompense you for a little over a month in hiding and – what did you call it? – wholesale slaughter to follow?'

'In the circumstances, it will have to,' said Amanda harshly.

'Needs must,' Porson agreed. He turned to the woman. 'And you'll come with me,' he said softly.

'No, I don't think so. I'll make up a story somehow.'

'To account for three dead bodies?'

'Yes, I'll tell them just what you suggested about your killing Jamie, and I'll say Mr Maitland and Mr Conway came with all kinds of accusations against me, because they were desperate at the thought of Richard being convicted. The police will believe me, I'll make them.'

'It seems the lady would rather do anything than go with you, Mr Porson,' said Antony. 'But I think she's wrong, you know, and it makes me wonder –'

'What?' asked Porson sharply when he broke off.

'You can't force her to go with you,' said Antony thoughtfully, 'and anyway she'd prove too much of a handicap. But I wonder just how much the police will believe of that story of hers. If they don't believe it and really get down to questioning her . . . how much does she know about your proposed escape route, Mr Porson?'

'Too much,' said Porson, and turned sharply towards Amanda. And as he moved Chris's hand went behind him and one of the potted plants – an azalea – went flying through the air. It struck Porson squarely on the side of the head, the gun went off, and Jamie turned, hiding his face against Maitland, as Amanda Hargreaves, with blood spurting from a wound in her breast slid slowly to the floor.

But before that happened Chris had charged. He aimed a kick at the hand that held the gun and the weapon flew harmlessly away into a corner of the room. Antony disengaged himself from Jamie; by the time he joined the struggle Chris was well on top but Porson was fighting like a demon. The next few moments after he had joined the scrum were never very clear in Maitland's memory. He had wrenched his shoulder within the first minute, and sickened by the waves of pain remembered afterwards only dimly that Jamie had possessed himself somehow of the cord that worked the venetian blinds — but what proper boy didn't carry a pen-knife upon his person? — and joined the fray himself, clinging like a limpet to the gunman's legs until finally he stopped struggling and they were able to tie him up.

Maitland struggled to his feet again and dropped into the nearest chair, while Chris after a quick look in his direction crossed the room to where Amanda Hargreaves lay. Porson was swearing steadily, so that it occurred to Antony vaguely through the waves of pain that were still washing over him that perhaps he ought to rouse himself to persuade Jamie to go out of the room. He was vaguely aware that Chris had gone down on his knees beside Amanda, but at that same moment, as though on cue, there came a thunderous knocking on the door.

Sunday, 9th February

'After that,' said Antony, 'it was all over bar the shouting. And there was a good deal of that, as a matter of fact,' he added reminiscently. It was teatime the following Sunday and the usual party was assembled, Roger and Meg, who would be staying on to dinner, and Sir Nicholas and Vera who would be leaving later for a concert and dinner in town.

'I can well imagine it,' said Sir Nicholas austerely and shuddered a little at the thought. 'Did you find the police difficult to convince?'

'Well, Chris and I spent the whole night making statements,' Antony admitted. 'But there was no mistaking Porson, he didn't even try to deny who he was, and though we didn't see him again after they took him away I gather that he sang like a canary.'

Sir Nicholas opened his mouth to remonstrate at this distortion of the English language, but Meg was before him. 'What I want to know, darling,' she said, 'is, was this Hargreaves woman dead?'

'No, the bullet had struck her a little higher than either Chris or I thought at first, only a little below the shoulder. That's why there was so much blood.'

'The situation appears to have been sordid in the extreme,' said Sir Nicholas, recovering himself. 'I cannot think why it is that whenever you go to Arkenshaw –'

'He's quite safe now, Uncle Nick,' said Jenny quickly.

Sir Nicholas regarded his nephew with some disfavour;

185

Antony's shoulder had been bound up tightly, and for once he had given in to the doctor's advice and had his arm in a sling. 'Yes, my dear,' said Sir Nicholas, 'and I suppose we must all be grateful for that. But –'

'Nothing else to be done,' said Vera, 'once the boy had telephoned.'

Sir Nicholas took his time to look around him. 'If you're all of you in league against me,' he said, 'I suppose I must refrain from further comment.' Antony caught Jenny's eye at that moment and grinned; they both of them knew that was the last thing that was likely to happen.

'Well, what had happened to Amanda Hargreaves?' asked Roger. 'You may as well finish the story properly, now you've started.'

'She's under arrest and in the prison hospital. It'll be a couple of weeks, I should think, before she's able to appear in court. And from what I observed of the lady she'll spend the time thinking of some good story to tell, but I very much doubt if it'll get her anywhere.'

'And your client?'

'Chris and Bushey can see to the formalities when the trial resumes. Jamie is with him and Star until his father is released, which will be tomorrow morning when Anderson tells the court that the prosecution don't propose to proceed any further with the matter. And to set your minds at ease,' he added, looking deliberately from Vera, to Meg, and then to Jenny, 'he's young, he'll get over it –I don't think he was over-fond of Aunt Amanda, though he always paid lip-service to her kindness, and once he's with his father again . . . I daresay he'll dine out on the story for the rest of his life.'

'The thing I want to know,' said Meg, 'is were you deliberately trying to get this man Porson to shoot her, darling? Because if you were I think it was very clever of you but just a tiny bit ruthless.'

'When it comes to a question of kill or be killed –' Roger began.

'Yes, I know all about that, darling, but it's Antony we're talking about. He isn't as sensible as you are. Is that what you intended?' she insisted.

'I realised the possibility, of course,' said Antony, speaking slowly and thinking it out as he went. 'But if it's any excuse for my actions, Meg, I felt responsible for Jamie, and for Chris as well. I hoped really just to distract Porson's attention, to give Chris a chance to make a move.' He smiled reminiscently. 'He was magnificent, you know. I'd tipped him off that I'd try to give him an opportunity, though I admit I was afraid he'd make his move too soon. But when it came to the point he played up pretty much as well as you'd have done, Roger. Does that answer your question, Meg?'

'Yes, darling, I think it does,' said Meg. She smiled seraphically around the assembled company. 'I told you it was all a question of jealousy, didn't I? If you'd listened to me –'

'What then?' asked Antony, amused.

'All this needn't have happened,' said Meg. 'You see, I quite agree with Uncle Nick, you shouldn't get mixed up in the kind of thing that's going to be dangerous, even to oblige a friend.'

'Now look here, Meg, that's a bit thick,' Roger protested. 'Don't you remember – ?'

'I never forget anything –'

'You might as well claim to be a female elephant,' muttered Antony mutinously.

'– and that time you were just as much to blame as Antony was, perhaps even more so. And it isn't fair to worry Jenny.'

'Didn't know anything about it until it was over,' said Vera in her gruff way. 'Did you Jenny?'

'I knew Antony was worried. The rest wouldn't have occurred to me,' she added, tilting her chin a little and giving Sir Nicholas what for her was a positively malignant look, 'if Uncle Nick hadn't made all that fuss about

187

his accepting a brief out of town. It wasn't a bit sensible, Uncle Nick, you know it wasn't.'

Sir Nicholas, who had been quietly sipping his tea while this exchange was going on, put down his cup and eyed his niece for a moment as though he'd never seen her before. 'My dear child,' he said, 'if you can't recognise a clear case of precognition when you see one –'

'Precognition nothing!' Maitland was moved to protest. 'You know as well as I do, Uncle Nick, you only complained about my going to Arkenshaw because you couldn't think of anything else to grouch about. As it happened –'

'As it happened, I was right,' said Sir Nicholas placidly. 'The whole affair was botched and mismanaged, but that's nothing new and was only what I expected. However, all's well that end's well –'

'That's the wrong play, Uncle Nick,' Jenny told him.

'– and I think on this occasion even Antony won't be able to summon up too much sympathy for the guilty party.'

'Cold-blooded,' said Vera, nodding.

'I should think not indeed,' Meg agreed. 'You won't, will you darling?' she demanded.

'No,' said Maitland, a little too emphatically. He glanced across at Jenny, who perhaps of all of them realised most clearly that the answer to that question couldn't possibly be a clear-cut yes or no. 'I don't suppose Chris has an endless string of friends likely to find themselves in trouble with the law,' he went on, and whether he was reassuring her or himself it was impossible to say. 'In any case, I'm home again, and you didn't turn the house upside down while I was away as so often happens, and I think that's something both Uncle Nick and I are very grateful for, whatever Vera may think. But I think possibly – just possibly, Uncle Nick – the next time an out-of-town brief comes along I'll listen to your advice.'

'May I live to see the day,' said Sir Nicholas piously. But it must be admitted that neither he nor Vera, when they discussed the matter later, expressed any great optimism.